CROSSING THE GULF

Crossing the Gulf

Stories by

Keith Harrison

OOLICHAN BOOKS
LANTZVILLE, BRITISH COLUMBIA, CANADA
1998

Canadian Cataloguing in Publication Data

Harrison, Keith,
   Crossing the gulf

ISBN 0-88982-167-4
   I. Title.

PS8565.A656C76 1998   C813'.54   C97-911113-7
PR9199.3.H348C76 1998

We acknowledge the support of the Canada Council for the Arts for our publishing programme.

THE CANADA COUNCIL | LE CONSEIL DES ARTS
FOR THE ARTS | DU CANADA
SINCE 1957 | DEPUIS 1957

Grateful acknowledgement is made to the BC Ministry of Tourism, Small Business and Culture for their financial support.

We acknowledge the financial support of the Government of Canada through the Book Publishing Industry Development Program for our publishing activities.

Published by
Oolichan Books
P.O. Box 10, Lantzville
British Columbia, Canada
V0R 2H0

Printed in Canada by
Hignell Printing Limited
Winnipeg, Manitoba

Acknowledgements

A number of these stories have been published or are forthcoming in the following magazines: "Rain in the Laurentians" in *Fiddlehead;* "Near Big Timber" in *Event;* "Tennis at Popham Beach" in *Canadian Author & Bookman* (Okanagan Short Story Award); and "The Malcolm Lowry Professional Development Grant" in *The Capilano Review.*

for Jo
and for the friends
who read these stories early
and made them better
than I could have imagined.

Contents

Crossing the Gulf

At Parksville, the tide was out. Beneath the early morning mist the ridged dunes stretched out to the blue-black sea. The red car was headed south on the Island Highway. He glanced across at her, pushed down the accelerator a bit, and said, "Wondering about your students?"

She laughed, turned off the radio, saying, "No, my kids can survive a day without me. Watch the speed limit in town. I was only thinking about last night's dream."

Their car passed a logging truck, just before the double lanes became one for the short steel bridge.

"I dreamed I was vomiting up letters. They were all

kinds, with a lot of sharp Ks and Qs. And all of them were capital letters—about the size of the fridge magnets my sister's kids have. I was squatting below this magnificent arbutus that twisted up from a cliff high above a bay, you know, the huge kind of tree with wild branches in every direction that has been here since before Columbus—six hundred years of living or more—and I was throwing up Alphabet Soup!"

"It sounds like the nightmare of an English teacher."

"Letters were lying all over the moist ground, scattered on green salal leaves, flung up onto the lower boughs of fir, stuck to the exposed roots of the arbutus. And my throat hurt like . . . like that dragging needle in rap music, that scratch scratch rhythm. And I was upchucking all the letters needed for words like 'quick' and 'kite' and 'exit'. There were more than enough piling up to spell all three of my own names twice!"

"Jean Pamela Theopolous. Jean Pamela Theopolous."

"I was kneeling on my bare knees on cedar boards on the edge of a deck, with all these puked up letters mounting in front of my eyes, and I began noticing— like the English teacher I am—words forming in the air as several letters in a row would fly out of my mouth, like 'm-a-d', and even in my dreams I was enough of a grammarian to ponder the level of diction, wondering if I was getting 'angry' or going 'crazy', while all the time watching to see if a longer word like 'madam' or 'madrona' might emerge. In a weird way I was looking forward to my next vomit."

"Do you know why the arbutus tree, or 'madrona', is called the tourist tree in Mexico?"

12

"Wait. I'm not finished telling you my dream."

"Because it's red and peeling."

"Good joke, but maybe my dream is some parable about being a tourist on this continent, colonization, say, making those already here talk our phonemes. Why else was I puking out scads of letters? And only English ones—none from your Greek alphabet, no Cyrillic letters, and forget Farsi. Just the same, everyday, twenty-six, garden-variety English letters, making me gag. Look, Nick, yon construction project has a *lien* and hungry look."

"How can you joke about that, Jean? They still owe us the final payment of $20,000!"

"You don't like the cut of my gibes? Sorry, I'm a little hyper. Has a date been set yet for the bankruptcy hearing?"

"The eleventh of next month, but I won't hold my breath."

"But the housing you built must be worth enough to cover their debt?"

"There are a lot of people waiting, pushing in line. Tell me the rest of your dream, Jeannie."

"Did you ever hear a comedy sketch by Bob Newhart about how an infinite number of monkeys working away on an infinite number of typewriters would write billions and billions of pages of nonsense, but, eventually, and by pure chance, all of Shakespeare and every other conceivable book?"

"You don't need monkeys. A computer could do it faster, but who's got the time to read them all to find out which one in a trillion makes any sense?"

"In my nightmare I couldn't figure out how to keep my lunch down, or why there was no visible evidence of it, so I stepped off the deck onto the wet earth, nearer to the bluff and the ocean, searching for clues, hoping to find bites of my Granny Smith apple, bits of cheddar cheese, maybe crumbs from the Stoned Wheat Thins, but there were only heaps of letters that were spongy to touch—and surprisingly heavy to pick up and heave over the cliff edge. With muddy fingers, I leaned on a split-rail fence, looking at the smooth sea far below. Even in my dreams, Nicky, I eat no animals, swallow no flesh, slaughter no living thing."

"What about the cow held prisoner for years to make the milk that's then stolen for your cheese and crackers?"

"Why did I ever marry you? It must have been your beard that made you look so wise."

"Look?"

"Don't you like that idea of letters as digested food? Talking is a little like feeding someone."

"You mean like mother birds—or teachers—chewing on worms, then spitting them down the throats of their young? Hey, Jeannie, stop hitting me. These corners are slippery."

"We'll make the seven o'clock ferry easily. Here's Nanaimo, 'the place where peoples meet,' according to the Indians."

"I thought it was 'the place where the tribes fight.'"

"Don't tailgate that truck, please. In my dream, as—thanks—as I was leaning over the cedar fence, four eagles . . ."

"That split-rail fencing from red cedar is almost impossible to find now, and costs a fortune."

"I just learned that the word 'paradise' means

14

'walled garden' in Old Persian. Do we dream of fencing nature in, or of walling people out?"

"Both, but I'm just the driver, madam. You were saying about 'four eagles'?"

"Four eagles circled my head, making throaty, melodic sounds, when I started to vomit again, sending letters sailing down the cliff like playing cards, flipping and turning in the air. The eagles floated out over the ocean while my alphabet bounced off the conglomerate rock that shelved way out—but no letters reached the clear green pools of the bay itself."

"I'm going to go this way."

At the green arrow the car turned left off the Island Highway and cut down Departure Bay Road.

"And all of a sudden, Nicky, my body was over the cedar fence, flipping and turning in the cool ocean wind, and the letters screaming from my mouth came out linked and written in blood—then were blown separate and vague, and I couldn't read them fast enough. I was about to be battered against the sloping rock-face that glared in the sun when the alarm woke me. I got up and had a large glass of water, dressed, climbed into the car for the ride to the ferry, and lived happily ever after."

"Sweetheart."

"Do you have the money?"

He shook his head.

"Falling in brightness to certain death, Nick—seeing your descent all the way down, as in my dream, doesn't scare me like falling blackly—not knowing when to expect the stone hardness. But I'd much rather glide with the eagles, or land alive in the saltwater and swim my way to shore! It's only quarter to seven."

As the car stopped at the glass booth, she handed the driver a fifty-dollar bill, which he passed on to the unsmiling figure in a dark-blue uniform. The attendant returned some change, saying, "Lane number seven."

"Jean, do you feel like stretching your legs before we board the ferry?"

"Sure, if you'll give me a hug."

Together, they set off towards the terminal building, but did not go inside. They walked around its outside walls and stood near some wooden picnic tables, by the edge of the sea. There were views of Newcastle Island's green forest, the wide, half-calm waters of Departure Bay, the wavetops torn white in the Gulf of Georgia, and the snowy Coast Range beyond, high and still.

"Why don't we just swim across, Jean?"

"You, silly. Didn't you hear the announcement to 'return to your vehicle?'"

While they were hurrying back to their car, traffic started curving up the high entrance ramp to the tall ferry, several motorcycles with bundled bodies in the lead. A double-trailer truck with planed lumber rolled heavily onto the lower deck. Nick unlocked the car door for her. "We could cover every inch of our bodies in creosote or something, like on the pilings, and just dive in."

Smiling up at him, she squeezed the underflesh of his lifted arm, ducked beneath, and sat down, then stretched away from him to pull up the lock button on the driver's door.

"The tide's going to turn against us soon," Nick said, "so we'd better get started. We don't have to swandive in. We could wade in one cold quarter-inch of skin at a time, if you're chicken. The distance across is not much more than the length of a marathon, and with the westerly blow out in the Gulf, we should be able to average about three miles an hour—could easily swim across to Passage Island or Point Atkinson before dusk."

He started the car engine. Their red car followed the line of vehicles over the paved parking lot, up the steep ramp, and onto the boat.

"Nick, if you're hungry, go ahead and have some breakfast. I'm quite happy reading."

"No, Jeannie, if you won't swim across the Gulf with me, let me tell you what you'll be missing, and then you'll want to swim back with me—and we can save fifty bucks on the ferry ticket."

They reached the top of the stairs that led up from the car deck, and paused. She caught her breath, and pointed to some plastic yellow-brown cushioned seats, sideways to the broad window that framed the ocean.

"Port, in case you get lost," Nick said. "We won't use flippers, and won't need plastic goggles because we'll develop sea eyes. But for the first little while our heads will bob in the waves as we swim out past the beaches of Newcastle Island, underneath the fir and arbutus trees, in water that is wonderfully buoyant and refreshing, and by the time we're swimming alongside the flank of Gabriola Island, our fingers will be webbed with skin."

"Yuck. Here we go!"

"From our backbones will bloom silver dorsal fins, and maybe for you a cute little fin by your anal pore, but your hair that looks so unbelievably black when it's wet will be unchanged, and when we get a bit chilled, a boil of herring will warm our bodies, and when we get glum, harbour seals will tickle us with their whiskers, and when we get lonely, shoals of fishes will nudge and cuddle us, and when we get tired, dolphins will carry us on their slippery rounded backs until we have the strength to swim on.

"At times seaweed will whip us in the face, and the very sound of the ocean will almost wear us out, and we won't be able to see land anywhere. The sun will go down behind a wall of snow, and we will suddenly realize we are swimming into winter, with ice clinging to our fins, and the sea around us freezing into a tundra.

"We're shivering and hungry, and trying to stand upright on our tailfins, but can't, toppling down on the hard, ragged polar ice as blackness comes to the blank tundra."

"I'm not going swimming with you again!"

"Leaving a creosote trail on the ice, we scrape forward under the Northern Lights, when a fat polar bear— a really well-fed polar bear—ambles forward under the magical sky, and tied around his furry and fat neck is a bottle of ouzo, and we slurp down its licorice warmth, and suddenly we are swimming in the soupy Mediterranean, and ripe olives from trees are falling into our mouths."

"O.K. I'll go swimming with you."

"Our exhausted, still-wriggling torsos swim on, together, slowing as we glide over a sunken city and gaze into dazzling stone architecture that flutters with each of our strokes, then we propel ourselves on, swimming for months around the capes of huge continents, and . . ."

"That's just Bowen Island out there."

"And we swim on, into the warm, paradisal Pacific . . ."

"With no Bikini Atoll."

"Wearing no bikini at all, and your black hair is as black as this sudden night at sea that we now try to swim through. In our blind paddling we bump into each other, and listen for the other's breathing mouth to take in bits of the starless midnight air, wondering at our stubbornness, asking ourselves how we are staying afloat, going mad in this black voyaging, when our sea eyes see—off at a great distance—a very tiny fire."

"Like Hero and Leander."

"We keep on swimming, and it's my story."

"'On Hellespont, guilty of true-loves' blood/In view and opposite, two cities stood/Sea-borders, disjoined by Neptune's might . . .'"

"We swim faster, but the fire goes out and we are lost, and we know we swim in circles, catching at each other's legs (for our tailfins have fallen off), tangling like slimy kelp with each other, and we're stone-certain we're drowning, but no longer care, when suddenly the fire flames forth again . . ."

"I like that alliteration."

"When this fucking fabulous fire flames forth again, and we swim on, but now with only our human arms and hearts—the skin webbing of our fingers has been shed. The fire, though bigger, looks too far away for our tired muscles and dub-glub hearts, but, all at once, there will be the wonderful smell of nearby cedar trees, and right before our briny eyes the Point Atkinson lighthouse will flash."

"I like the ending, Nick. Look at those whitecaps."

"Is that all? We've circumnavigated the globe!"

"What do you mean 'we,' Kemo Sabe?"

"Who were Hero and that girl?"

"'Hero' was 'that girl.' Don't you know your Greek myths? Leander fell in love with Hero, a kind of nun who worshipped Venus, and he swam nightly between Asia and Europe to be with her, guided by her fire. One night it blew out in a storm. Is that your stomach growling? We'd better order you some breakfast before our ferry gets there."

"No, I'm fine, love, but you look a bit, uh, greenish."

"'Green'? With envy of your story-telling skills? Or 'green' enough with ignorance to believe in your saga? Or 'green' with youth because you're an old coot, five years older than me? I'll tell you about 'green', as in 'chlorophyll'. It was raining, and this woman went into a gardening shop, and said, 'I can't make anything grow.' Now most gardening stores are greenhousy, with lots of glass and light, but this place was small and dingy, with dusty packets of seeds and flowers just past their bloom—not a hint of a bud."

"What happened to Hero and Leander?"

"Too late. The heroine of my story addresses the man behind the counter, Mr. Jackson. He is a small man, bald on top, with a fringe of long greasy black hair hanging in back down to his shoulders, like that passenger there—a kind of hirsute compensation, I guess."

"Keep your voice down, Jeannie, or you'll get me into a fight."

"She says to Mr. Jackson, 'I want to buy a green thumb.' He turns away, and walks through a narrow doorway to a cramped inner room with a dozen halogen lights hanging down from the ceiling. She's afraid to follow but decides to go and stand in the doorway. She watches him reach into an old fridge—past some chilled formal bouquets that seem funereal. Then Mr. Jackson takes out a large Grey's mustard jar, and she steps inside the too-illuminated back room, curious to see what happens when he unscrews the black lid. He sets the lid upside down on the metal sink edge—where chipped-off white paint reveals the dark cast iron—and measures out a quarter teaspoon of a yellowish liquid that looks not unlike mustard mixed with olive oil. This he funnels into a very tiny crystal perfume bottle. Mr. Jackson then tightly screws the mustard lid back on, and puts the jar back into the fridge. Next, he stands up on a three-legged stool, and stretches—precariously—to open a high cupboard door above the sink, removing a shimmering cobalt blue bottle that she recognizes as Auralgan, which she uses for her earaches. He hops down, and, using the dropper, squeezes seven drops into the miniature crystal bottle, then twists its lid on very tightly. He shakes it vigorously, and the liquid inside goes green. On a white dot of shiny paper he writes, '5.' He peels away the backing, and sticks this on the perfume jar, holding it out to her, saying, 'That will be a nickel.'

"Carefully, she holds the tiny object between thumb and forefinger, laughing, 'Only a nickel?' She knows this whole thing is absurd to begin with—an idle fantasy that she can buy some skills to keep her plants alive—but she slides a hand into her jeans pocket and sets a nickel down by one of the chrome taps. As she is wondering if this magical greenness should be applied externally or—ugh!—drunk, Mr. Jackson moves over to a wall bookcase, shoves aside some tall books about cacti, and reveals a grey-green wall safe. He clicks some numbers, swings the door wide open, and removes a can of Drano. It has no top, and from inside of it he plucks out a spice jar with the word, 'thyme' printed on its original label. But what she sees through the glass looks like roots hidden from the sun. These long, pale, straggly, wormy things are clumped together with a blackish elastic band. Mr. Jackson walks slowly over to the sink, picks up her nickel, spins it up into the bright air with his nicotined thumb, catches it deftly, then carefully positions it in the very centre of the thyme jar lid, before putting the Drano can, the spice bottle, and her nickel inside the safe. Swinging the door shut—it locks with a click—he announces, 'The antidote costs $20,000.'"

"I've heard that number before."

"She runs, and keeps on running, out of that back room, out of Mr. Jackson's florist shop into the rain, down the sidewalk, the length of several blocks, halting finally at an intersection, sodden, panting, waiting for the light to change, suddenly aware that . . . there's a seal out there."

"Where?"

"Look. There. He's just gone under."

"Why do you say 'he,' Jean?"

". . . suddenly she is aware that she has left her brand new red Honda Prelude parked in front of Mr. Jackson's."

"Couldn't you at least change the colour of our car?"

"She walks all the way back to the gardening shop, and drives off, soaked and exhausted, clenching the mysterious crystal jar in her fist. When she gets home, she wants to bury this vial in the bottom of a brown-paper garbage bag and put that bag inside a larger, dark-green plastic one. Her one wish in life becomes to rush this perfume bottle of green guck out of the house—toss it out back for the garbage truck to get rid of—but the *men* wouldn't be by to pick it up for three more days, and, anyway, she couldn't be so irresponsible as to just throw away something that might be worse than toxic waste, and which would likely end up in a landfill for some new suburb. And for similar environmental reasons she didn't want to just flush it down the toilet. Also, she was scared that the water might combine with the potion to create some chemical catastrophe. That was your stomach growling again. Why don't you get some food?"

"What happens next? I bet Jeannie lets the genie out of the bottle."

"Taking a deep breath, she tells herself not to over-react. Some charlatan, or, more likely, a joker, has sold her some harmless green goop, for a nickel! She'll just follow her first impulse, and chuck it. She even opens the cream-painted cupboard door beneath her porcelain sink, extends an arm inside, and is about to drop the perfume bottle on top of coffee grinds and a star-fished banana peel. She stares at the PVC plumbing—installed by a frequent subcontractor to Nikos Theopoulos Limited who phoned me yesterday about an N.S.F. cheque . . ."

"It will clear now, now that I've cashed the Svendsens' second payment. But where the hell does George get off, calling my wife at home about our business arrangements? That's the last . . ."

"She hears this voice in her head. It is high-pitched and buzzy—one she has never heard before—which asks, 'What if it works?' She has never had a mystical

23

experience, she has never believed in magic (that she can remember), but, she thinks, there may be inexplicable forces of growth and healing that it would be close-minded to reject without trying. She loosens the tiny cap, one counter-clockwise twist. The dentist's office also called yesterday to remind you of Friday's appointment."

"You're worse than TV commercials with your interruptions."

"She pauses, for suspense, and to irritate Nick who has predicted that a green genie will jump out of the tiny crystal jar. She tells herself not to be silly, and quickly unscrews the lid, lifts it off, and nothing happens. She starts to laugh, and, still grasping the tiny lid between her thumb and forefinger, she sets the open bottle down by the phone and picks up the kettle, fills it with water, and puts it on the stove. Out of a canister she gets some loose green tea, and with her left hand scoops some into a ball-mesh—what's the word for those metal tea things?"

"Metal tea things."

"As she's waiting for the water to come to a boil, she notices the shot-glass of wooden toothpicks. By a kind of magnetic force her right hand takes out a toothpick, and then her body feels as if it is being dragged across the tiled floor with the tiny wooden pointer held in front of her chest until, above the vial, the toothpick dips like a dowser's forked stick, plunging down into the small aperture in the perfume bottle. She hears some tiny bubbles quietly pop, then nothing. The toothpick she lifts out drips a gummy green, and—all at once—becomes a sprig of parsley. Her first thought is that she has had bad breath lately, and this is the cure. Then she remembers her grandmother used to grow some parsley near the garage, and it was the first thing she had ever tasted straight from a garden, so strong-flavoured and crunchy fresh—afterwards she had felt like Popeye with his spinach: invincible.

"She holds this parsley sprig like a wand, her left hand still pinching the tiny perfume cap, while the kettle boils like mad and on the counter is this jar of mutant chlorophyll, open. She needs to get the lid back on the bottle *right away*, but is afraid to put this extoothpick down. The steam burns into her face while she is screwing back the little lid with her left hand. The perfume bottle begins to spin, teeters, and smashes down on the brown tiles, spilling out from its broken glass something that looks like green molasses.

"Between her feet a pale green shoot rises, thickens, becomes a huge stem that shoots up so quickly she needs to step back to protect her crotch. Her face jerks up to watch the broad leaves press against the ceiling, spread outward in all directions, reach to the edges of the four walls and start down. The ceiling's white paint disappears under a layer of wild greenness. Tendrils now darken the windows. She squeezes her eyes shut, thinking, This is not happening to me, it's only a bad dream from which I will now awake. Opening her eyes, she finds the door—now almost completely hidden beneath clustering leaves and ropey branches—is tied shut. She panics, grabs a bread knife and races for the front door, tearing and sawing and hacking and ripping. Tugging at the knob, she gets the door open a few inches, squeezes free and runs down the front steps. Lunging into the car, she careens down the block, afraid to glance behind at her house filling with something like cancer.

"At Mr. Jackson's she double-parks her *red* car, and bursts inside. Among the gloom and wilting plants, he is nowhere to be seen. She pushes open the narrow door to the back room, and there, underneath the halogen noonday, he is waiting for her, one hand on the combination knob. She gives him the keys to her one-year-old Honda Prelude, and he twists the dial, swings open the door to the safe, and pulls out the spice jar. In her hands it is surprisingly weightless."

"Does Mr. Jackson know there are five years of car payments still to be made?"

"As she runs outside, he shouts after her, 'Make sure you get the roots.' There is a taxi cruising by, and she gets in and is back home in minutes, only to see branches sprouting from the chimney, reaching like crooked brown arms into the sky, and a dense greenness pushing at the living room's wide window—bulging it. As she swivels out of the taxi, a green fist breaks through the glass with a terrifying CRACK! The taxi driver guns off without his fare, and she's left at the curb to gape at these green tentacles coming across the lawn at her."

"You mean like this?"

"Nick. Stop. That woman's getting up to move. She thinks you're a hairy squid."

"And what's wrong with that?"

"Standing on the curb, she unscrews the lid of the spice jar, pulls out the clump of seven soggy root-like/worm-like entities, tears off the old elastic band, and hurls one of the damp noodle things at a light-green, new-born leaf that has come from the darkly massed exploding greenness of the house and that now touches her left running shoe. There's a little shrivelly cry as the leaf turns grey, and the whole branch wilts—nearly all the way back to the front window. She follows, through the whiff of burning vegetable matter, stepping on charred cellulose, broken window glass, getting closer to The Source. She hurls a root-worm thing at the window frame that is choked by a malignant green. An entire jungle writhes in the fixed rectangle, shrinking, blackening, but still blocking her way back inside. Throwing a root-worm—and another right after that—she watches all the colour leach from the exfoliation in the window space. Breathing in a kind of death-dust, she kicks at the sooty web of branches, and leaps down inside the humid darkness that was her home. Gagging, using a fifth worm-root-noodle, she zaps her way forward, towards the kitchen. All this while branches shriek, fall from the ceiling, and one hits her right shoulder, making her drop everything except for the last of the noodley antidotes. Her eyes burn with thick, gritty smoke, as her ears are pierced by ululating."

"Ululating?"

"An Arabic wailing cry, used in liner notes on jazz albums. She crawls on her hands and knees, getting hints of the earth-coloured Mexican tiles under the debris, her sore eyes trying to fix on the massive tree trunk still five feet away. Ignoring the flashing pains from her shoulder, she clambers over an enormous branch, rips ashen leaves from her eyes. In her 'blind swimming,' or her 'black voyaging' . . . which was it?"

"Both."

"In her near-blind voyaging, she flails desperately

27

forward, falling against the base of the tree, her thumb squishing the last wormy noodle deep into the scaly bark.

"With a gargantuan slurping noise, the tree disappears down into the wet grout between two tile squares, and a fine haze of green drifts down from the ceiling, and she lives happily ever after."

"Where did you get that idea from?"

"Aside from the obvious—and my jade plant that's been ailing ever since I moved it to the northern light of the living room—there is a story I've been teaching called 'The Chaser,' written by John Collier fifty or sixty years ago, that has a magic potion. Do you know what power it gives?"

"The King Midas touch?"

"Instant and total love from anyone you want. The antidote is an expensive poison."

"Why would anyone want an antidote?"

"Think about it a little."

"You scare me. Do you want to go outside for a walk on the deck?"

"Sure. The sun's come out, and the wind's dying down. Do I really look green?"

"I exaggerated, but some fresh air might do you some good. I hope the guys at the site are doing some work today."

"How's it going?"

"A few more days to lock-up, and a third payment. Do you want to sit out here by the lifeboats?"

"Let's walk around to the bow."

"Did I ever tell you the story of the husband and wife who loved each other?"

"Come on, Nick. Can't you invent a plausible story?"

"Did I ever tell you the one about the husband and wife who had never once made love to each other? Their names were Leslie and Terry."

"Who's female?"

"Hero. Leslie and Terry dreamed only of making love to someone like Mick Jagger or Madonna."

"Leslie is female?"

"Leslie had a great set of . . . testicles."

"Keep your voice down, Nick. Let's sit out here in the sun and the wind—pretend we're captains of this ship. 'Avast, me hearties!' Do you know what 'avast' means?"

"It means, 'to prepare for standing a long night-watch by filling at least half a galvanized gallon bucket with fresh urine.'"

"Shhh!"

"What is this? Censorship? Wait. I'll take my coat off, and we can sit on it, and lean our backs against this wall."

"Sir Nicholas Raleigh."

"O.K.? Leslie, this husband, and Terry, this wife, or was it the other way around?"

"Nick!"

"It's Sunday morning anyway. They're still in bed, sitting under a pulled-up quilt, letting the surface tension of a week evaporate from their skins. They're drinking *café au lait*, a tape plays balalaika music, and the glass door of the balcony is slid open a crack, letting in a warm breeze—like this one—only—in the air of the story—there is a scent of lemons. If she weren't his wife, he would set down his cup and kiss the lovely crevice behind her folded knees, slip his tongue inside her glistening pink mouth, rub his stubbly chin under her slick armpits, taste the bitter-sweet between the between of her legs. She would drag her ten fingernails down the long, muscled length of his back, massage his tanned runner's calves, pinch his jade plant ear lobes, and tongue his buttery asparagus stalk, if he weren't her husband."

"Can you lower your voice?"

"No one's here, just now. Then, from outside, there is a sharp rap. On the far side of their sliding glass door, they see another couple. These two are total strangers, but, of course, they have two eyes each, toes protruding from sandals, a pair of hands—they are almost familiar. But what are they doing there, or is it here?

"To his horror, his wife gets off the bed, moves towards the sliding door, the smooth melon-halves of her bum . . ."

"First asparagus, now melons. You're just hungry, Nick."

". . . moving to welcome them *in*. He wraps the quilt—or is it 'guilt?'—around his naked body, and runs to hide in the bathroom, where he sits on the potty in disbelief.

"To make sure he's not just dreaming this up, he peeks out from behind the bathroom door."

"What? There are no key-holes in the modern locksets you install?"

"He sees his wife on top of this strange woman, her face far away, lost between coffee-coloured legs, while standing next to Terry's succulent ass is the red-haired stranger, his dick like a totem pole."

"Mixed metaphor."

"Like a critic, outside the performance, he watches the moving haunches of the two women—though still

30

anxious about the other guy in *his* bedroom—until he begins aching for the feel of his stripped body pressed against another's hungering flesh, with all these openings opening, and for the first time in his life he wishes he had two asparaguses.

"But then Leslie thinks, as the strange man with fiery pubic hair starts to caress Terry's delicious half-melons, What about AIDS? This could be a plot to kill them! There are no condoms even in the bedside table. Dripping with jealousy, pearling with lust, he rushes into the bedroom, beside himself. The two women begin to cry out in pleasure, are ululating, and he wants to plunge into some key hole . . ."

"Shh."

"We should be at Passage Island in about thirty-five minutes. It's getting hot out here."

"Torrid, nearly."

"To continue, Leslie grabs the two marvellous melon-halves and rolls his wife off the other woman who has swollen breasts, milky-wet from nursing . . ."

"Now it's infantile, on top of racist and sexist."

"You think desire is politically correct? You told me (two years later) that you fell in love with me for the way I *smelled*."

"You still smell wonderful to me."

"As this strange woman sits astride him, he remembers his unfinished *café au lait*, and delights in her bony legs and unknown moles, while she revolves like the world, and shining in the crevices in back of his wife's knees is sweat that his tongue tastes, as a male tongue bathes his shoulder. Then they go at it, like four starving eagles. Inside his head, lights swing together, smash, and explode, and he can no longer tell if he is taking

31

or taken, evil or good, married or unmarried, milking or being milked, male or female, dying or being born, Terry or Leslie."

"When you make love to me, Nick, and you close your eyes, are you imagining another woman?"

"No way, Jeannie. Why would I think of anyone else?"

"You just did."

"I was just making up a story. If I had some ideal Form that I looked at in my brain during lovemaking, it would be like jerking off, or even worse, Platonic! And you know I love hugging this body of yours. Let's go for a longer stroll around the boat, and I'll tell you a true story."

"All stories are true, psychologically, and any other kind of truth is hard to get to."

"This is a true romance. She wore a polka-dot sweater. It was almost seven years ago, on a Boeing 737, waiting for take-off at the Vancouver Airport. She was sitting in his window seat, so he took out his boarding pass to show her. She unclicked her seatbelt, but then he said it didn't matter, she might as well stay where she was. He was on his way to Ottawa for the funeral of his unloved step-mother.

"As the plane curved out over the sea, he glanced at her black hair and dark-brown eyes. He felt so fragile he could cry.

"With no one like a parent left alive, he had this absurd sense of being an orphan at thirty-seven. From the air the muddy Fraser River seemed unmoving. Was it only out of politeness that he had asked her what she did for a living?

"She had answered, 'I'm a giraffe wrangler.' All at once, it seemed, light had touched the greens of the geometric fields below, and he talked about how the broad patchwork of shades below was like a thin quilt his mother had once made, which really should be tacked up on a wall, but he couldn't help using it to keep his bed cosy—despite its fraying thinness.

"She explained she didn't like telling strangers she was an English teacher because then they began talking to her in an uptight way. She told him she was headed to Ottawa because she was sort of engaged to a chemical engineer who tested bridges for corrosion.

"When the stewardess came by with breakfast, they were talking so softly to each other, she thought they were together. There's Point Atkinson lighthouse."

"Your stomach's growling again, and both of us were hungry then. Remember? You traded your sausages for my scrambled eggs. Very symbolic, but I didn't mention it at the time!"

"I remember these snakey lakes glinted below, and we both agreed it would be foolish to turn down free drinks."

"I liked the way your eyes listened to me, and the way your voice came into the near gaps of speech, and I loved the way you smelled when you leaned over to look down at the sharp peaks of the Rockies."

"I was more disturbed by the strips of snow being blown away into the empty sky, and by the way you pushed out some polka dots. Who was the first to suggest we deplane at Calgary, and catch the very next flight back to the Coast?"

"You said you'd feel dumb asking a giraffe wrangler to marry you."

"And you told me to stick my neck out. There's the point for Horseshoe Bay."

"Good Luck!"

"We'd better get back to our car now."

At the top of the stairwell, he holds the heavy door open, and then they descend the ringing stairs to the car deck, where each puts a foot up on a shallow metal ledge, and looks over the single round railing at the churning water, as the boat slides into the dock under the mountains. He takes out his keys and goes to the driver's door. He looks back to see her spine bent way over, her long black hair drifting sideways, below and beyond the white railing.

"Jeannie, come on. It's time."

She flings her head backwards, snapping the hair against her shoulder blades, then turns and walks slowly to the red car.

"Did I ever tell you, Nick, that once upon a time, in a land far far way, this woman lost her lips?"

"No."

"Kissing. Where does it start? Before she could say a word like 'lipsss', or even hear that word, she knew she had them. Two of them had always been there: inside the womb, then nursing at her mother's breast. But one day they're gone from her face."

"Put your seat belt on."

"She was left with just a mouth. It wasn't like a wound, bloody and messy, but as if some surgeon had performed a textbook operation, and everything had healed perfectly."

"Love, we're driving off."

"Was it from kissing too many people too many times? Had her lips worn out like the stone steps of Canterbury Cathedral, which had been trod upon by too many feet—not of pilgrims, but by countless tour-

34

ists visiting her lips, overstaying their welcome? Had it been the reception lines at weddings, or greeting 'hello' at airports, or the drunken lurch of New Year's Eve's kisses, or the accumulated years of birthday parties, or the combined pressure of all those casual occasions silently erasing her lips? Or was it from days and nights of hard desire moistening against another's lips, breath after heavier breath, in a passionate symmetry of two lips that were one mouth on two lips that were another mouth and the same one? Tasting the riddle of their origins in kisses—like two innocent parents—who might scatter their genes together in one twice-loved grab-bag, a two-lipped self."

"Like red tulips are your two lips. Hey! I love your kisses, but not while I'm passing a bus."

"No, she feared, the problem had been not *enough* loving, and too few kisses. Once when I was twelve, he didn't know how, and I didn't either, but had wanted to learn—needed to find out—and I mashed my mouth into his, and heard the grinding of our teeth, and when, embarrassed, he turned away, holding his hand on his mouth, I tasted blood on my upper lip."

"I'm jealous of your twelve-year-old boyfriend."

"You should be. I wanted him to push his lips—their soft, clover-sweet hardness—against my mouth flesh again, and forever, but he walked away, a finger scrunching up the corner of his mouth, like he had been slugged. When you scratch your head fast, Nick, I know you're angry."

"I can still get retroactively jealous, you know."

"You're so smoochable, you don't have to worry. . . . Happy now? So, once upon a time, this woman lost her lips. She doubted they had fallen off on some

35

grey sidewalk. No one had come running after her, politely, in triumph, with voice raised, 'Excuse me, Lady, you appear to have dropped your lips.' Raising an index finger, she traced an ellipse over the smooth skin where her lips should have been. No, she had not yet become like her aged father who paced around the living room rug, demanding, 'Where are my reading glasses?'—when they were dangling from a black cord around his scrawny neck. She *really* didn't have any lips. Movie titles like *Kiss of the Spider Woman, Kiss Me Deadly, Stolen Kisses* flitted through her head. Was there a stolen kiss to account for the loss of her lips? She tried to remember who (whom) she had last kissed. Could a detective help solve this mystery? Or, in an unexpected plot twist, would she be exposed as the criminal: someone who had shamefully committed lipicide? And what, if anything, had liposuction to do with this? Because she had grown tired of male blathering, was this punishment for acting too lippy?"

"Yes."

"Had her lips somehow been absorbed into one of the thousands of reproductions of Marilyn Monroe's lips by Andy Warhol? Or Madonna's, which was worse—or perhaps better because she was still alive, and therefore her lips were maybe retrievable. What about the cowboy lips of the Marlboro Man? They didn't look like hers, but neither did any of the red lipsticky lips that had sold millions of cars.

"Nick, have you ever had the impulse just to put your lips on the man or woman sitting beside you on the subway or bus?"

"My lips are sealed, but I do remember a black-haired woman on a Boeing 737."

"Once I had to stop myself from kissing the fur of a wonderful seeing-eye dog. In this world it's better to kick or kill than to show affection."

"This isn't the sixties! Be realistic. Anyone could have AIDS."

"That's a myth that it can be transmitted through kissing."

"Maybe, but who wants to take a chance? And anyway, a guy kissing strangers would be charged with assault."

"This woman, Sonya, who no longer had lips, watched as the woman with a pointy nose from the condo next door stepped out onto the balcony with a large watering can. Was she wearing *her* lips? Her back was turned, bending over some potted plant—hiding her head? Maybe, Sonya thought, she was the culprit, desiring the shape or size of lips that fitted the proportion of her face better. However, when the woman swung around to water the hanging fuchsias, it was evident those lips weren't Sonya's, and they were also too wide for the sharp little nose. But what if the lips were only the first beauty item, and she was going to get a perfect nose *next*? Sonya felt this was paranoid thinking, especially when the neighbour's three-year-old son skipped out on to the balcony. He had the same pointy nose, and wonderful chocolate eyes, with fine black eyelashes, and his uncombed hair flashed in the sun."

"Go on, Jeannie."

"It must have been the light flashing down on all those freighters waiting to get into Vancouver's harbour. Sonya decided to go to Chinatown, where, just behind Sunrise Market, she glided along a hallway that had the restful atmosphere of a funeral chapel and something of the same smell. A plump apple-cheeked woman in a floral dress who looked like Mother Goose stubbed out her cigarette in a jade ashtray and handed Sonya her card: 'I charge twenty-five dollars a day. And of course expenses.' Sonya told the private detective about the missing lips and gave a detailed history of her kissing. In a tough voice the Mother Goose dick asked Sonya, 'Where were you last night?'

"Nick, let's just turn off at the end of the bridge."

"We can't, love."

"Visit the aquarium? Have a picnic in Stanley Park?"

"Dr. Jackson."

"Sonya said she hadn't gone out. Except to visit a friend in the maternity ward. The detective asked her if she had ever kissed an ouch better, or a bruise, or a cut on any of the hundreds of hurtable places on a child's growing body. When Sonya whispered 'No,' Mother Goose walked to the window and pulled the shades up and opened the windows wide and air came drifting in with a kind of stale sweetness of automobile exhausts. The detective turned, and looked back across the room at Sonya: 'You'll find your lips glued to the Plexiglass that separated you from the tiny babies in incubators.'"

"That's unfair. I wanted kids too. You . . ."

"Sonya stopped at a bar and had a couple of lipless scotches. They didn't do her any good."

"You have your kids at school."

"On loan. And kissing your bruises better is only *almost* enough. And usually you're carrying the moon around in your pocket, and don't need my lips."

"They're only more tests."

"You know, I could be very bitter."

"Everything's going to be fine."

"I appreciate your going hungry with me, but I'm the only one here with cancer! Don't cry, Nicky. I won't be able to . . ."

"God, I love you."

"Just drop me off here at the clinic. Go eat something, and later I'll tell you what happens next."

Near Big Timber

The ice hit the car so hard Jesse shied away from the driver's window—scared the glass would shatter into his eyes. Leaning towards his father, he struggled to steer in the humongous wind that had broadsided their Rabbit. He could no longer tell where the new soft blacktop of the freeway ended and the unfenced fields began. The front windshield had become a weird shower curtain, thrashed at by frozen water—and it was June! His father's mouth twisted with words he couldn't hear. Jesse pumped the brake pedal lightly—even before his father started to jab a bent finger frantically down at the gearshift. Steering a bit towards what he thought was the side of the road, Jesse halted the car, except that they kept moving—battered by large white chunks—rocking sideways in this scary wind.

Adam tasted coconut in his mouth and listened to the huge massed nuggets pounding at the metal shell. In this noisy blankness that Thai lunch less than an hour ago in Billings (served by a white-shirted North American Indian) seemed a decade away. There was too much racket to talk to his son, or even to think about whether the car insurance would cover the paint damage. The afternoon light had gone without warning. And what about that large tanker truck they had passed five minutes before? Would it plough blindly into them and burst their lives into flames? Adam didn't feel like getting out into the pelting ice (though it might be a smart move). On his car roof the hail kept banging, and now there was a loud, strange hissing underneath them.

For Jesse, the sudden invisibility was like being taken underground into those dark connecting caves in South Dakota. His father—in a typical move—had first *suggested* the guided tour, then *insisted*, and Jesse had gone down so he wouldn't be teased as a wimp all the rest of the way to Kelowna. And afterwards, his father had wanted to be thanked! It seemed dumb to waste a whole day crouching their way through a bunch of damp caves, but it turned out not to have been too boring. On the colour-coded map in the parking lot the cave network had looked like those brain cells on "David Suzuki," bulges joined together by those long stringy things—dendrites. Down below the hot prairie sun, the air had smelled funny—stale—and there had been a constant sound of dripping. What was that hissing noise? His bald father wearing that dumb straw hat had smiled and talked like a tourist—had come on to the guide, someone called Cindy with pointy tits and a ponytail shoved through the back of her Bulls cap. ("He's too tall. Is he really your son?" "That's what his mother tells me.") Embarrassing to be related to him—and how could anyone be happy if they had no hair? Cindy had said the Indian skull at the bottom of the entrance shaft was probably a teenager's—someone who hundreds of years ago had stumbled into that deep hole hidden by a bush. Smashed like a hailstone. What was this hissing sound, and where was that white smoke coming from, and why was his father always shouting at him?

Adam (with two fingers on the door lever) calculated that the tanker truck would be on top of them just about now. He yelled again, "It's too dangerous here!" His son just sliced the air back and forth beside the curly black hair covering his right ear, signalling he couldn't hear a thing. Adam glanced over his shoulder. He couldn't see if a huge, very inflammable vehicle was going to whump the small Rabbit and burn them to hell in Montana. The brochure propped below the glove compartment had big white letters against the black background: CUSTER BATTLEFIELD. They should get out (even in their shorts and sandals) so they would not be killed in here. Outside, the loud storm still dented his car, a whitish fog was rising, and now (instead of the hiss) there was a rushing sound of water. Adam rolled the window down a crack, and freezing bits pinged inside. "Quick, quick. Pop-pop-pop very fast," Chief Two Moon had reported of the shooting. There was a flood of water swirling past the front tire; the hail must have been melting against the heat of the invisible, newly laid road. His face stung, and his eyes, half-shut, hurt. Adam jerked his head away. Heavy ice pellets hit his bare arm and sun-burnt knees before he could crank the glass back up. It was worse than Québec in winter (though even a francophone like Luc had envied their leaving). Glancing back at the rear windshield, Adam (chilled) couldn't see a thing. He squinted at condensation, ice, and fog. Chief Two Moon had said that the smoke from the rifles of the Sioux had looked like a great cloud.

Jesse twisted the ignition key off, but he couldn't hear any difference. A sharp rap on his right shoulder made him flinch—fling an elbow up for protection. Jesse stared at his father's taut face: bared teeth, large eye whites, the grey nostril hairs. The Indian skull on the rocky floor had looked yellowed and small. His father held both palms up, outward—his words pelted away by hailstones. Raging, Jesse itched his head against the carpeted roof—rubbing hard and remembering that first thwack of his father's hand long ago when he'd been in the back seat, when his father had been much, much bigger—not a twerp as he was now. Jesse's mother had protested against the blow—the unfairness.

They'd be stranded here all night, Adam felt, in the middle of nowhere (with wet electricals) because his son (who had foolishly turned off the ignition and was now busy trying to screw his skull through the closed sun-roof) never stopped to think about the fu-ture: the ravines, the gulches, the ridges of the battle-field. It was a harsh world out there Jesse had to sur-vive in, with a lot of casualties. Adam caught his son's puckery face turning away from his own and regretted lashing out at his only child. His fear was irrational

43

anyway: the car would start again. "I'm sorry," Adam screamed, but saw that his mouth was (inadvertently) spraying Jesse's shirt. And from the corner of his left eye Adam saw faint lights coming.

Jesse pulled free from the heavy hand on his shoulder. Then he watched the long curved silver body of a tanker truck flash past like a mirage—no more than an inch from their outside mirror. He kept looking at the small rectangle of a mirror with its rounded-off corners. Beyond it, there was, again, nothing visible. Once more Jesse felt his father's hand—this time squeezing his shoulder. He shrugged the fingers away. Maybe they had almost been killed, but Jesse wasn't going to forget that punch so fast. An accident, the guide had said. The yellowed skull so small.

They couldn't stay here, Adam knew, but it would be stupider to go on. In this hailstorm they had no good options. Their old lives (now thousands of miles of their car's exhaust away) were almost ghost-like. And they might never reach the place of their new lives (somewhere on Lake Okanagan he hoped). The signs at the battlefield site had read, "Do not step off the path," and "Watch for rattlesnakes." Jesse was shaking, but Adam understood he couldn't touch him. Before the white-out the radio station from Lethbridge, Alberta had been playing requests for songs about lovin', leavin', and cryin' (all the same experience finally?).

Jesse hated this constant fucking noise of ice smashing into the glass and metal. He hated carrying the letter in the pocket of his warm-up jacket in the gym bag—did not think he could wait. He simply wanted to be safe—and alone—inside a warm bright high-roofed space where the wooden floor—with its honey-polish—felt so springy he could take off from near the top of the key with the ball, its circling grooves and countless dimples filling his right hand. Such an airy weight of joy to plant his left foot, leap skyward, and dunk! Or take an inbound pass, risk a few dribbles—stutter-step!—and square up to the basket, give a quick head-fake, focus on the front rim, and release the jump-shot: the globe spinning up backwards before floating down through the hoop with the magical "snick" of pure net—not ice smashing into metal and glass and his head.

Adam was pretty sure the VW would start again, but they shouldn't try it just yet. They needed to wait it out and pray that no more ghostly trucks were coming. Anyway, he had wanted this trip to be a male bonding adventure (as well as a way of avoiding some moving expenses). "Bad news can be Good news," he would tell his clients when the market troughed, reminding them of opportunities to buy low, for investors who were smart. He looked across at his son who was no longer squirming, who seemed to be smiling to himself. The company had wanted to set up a new office in Kelowna, and in that fast-growing town there would be enough retirees and other transplants to pay for his dream house on the lake. Adam had needed to step smartly to win this transfer from headquarters in Montréal, and now their Anglo friends felt deserted. In a Banana Republic that couldn't grow bananas, who would want to be paid in Québecois dollars? Not that the Canadian one (leaden with debt) was any great shakes either. And French was much easier to learn than Mandarin, or whatever Asian language would be needed in B.C. Adam reached forward for the map which he had folded open. All these "B" places: Billings, Bozeman, Butte, and the town nearest to them (which would be a good nickname for his son), Big Timber.

Jesse liked the gym best during free shooting in practice—when the coach had gone for a smoke and there were only the players. Would the gym in Kelowna be in a separate building from the classrooms with their tiny desks, and teachers with tiny minds? Maybe the science guy would be O.K. Fake the hook shot, spin free, and, leaning inbounds, drive along the baseline before the defence could rotate, and stuff it in the hoop. Above their sloping garage roof, the rusting orange paint on the rim hadn't been absorbed into the metal, but the white latex had been sucked right into the plywood. In Kelowna maybe he could convince Dad to get a see-through glass backboard on a steel pole, and a wide, level driveway. At the games, the cutest girls would be in the stands, or on the sidelines cheerleading in flaring microskirts, watching his every move—if he got to play.

Next Monday, Adam thought, she would be flying out to B.C. (California North) in time for the house search, and he (guiltily) half-wished she were not coming. He was not yet too decrepit for all those babes he would meet. It was unfair, but how could he look forward to the prospect of decades of sex with a wrinkling face, drooping breasts, and the white stretch marks from Jesse that he should love? He couldn't break the news of a divorce (good-bye dream house on lake) to a son who was still troubled by adolescence, and hassled for being Anglo, and male, and white, and . . . no way his son was gay! Maybe all three of them should have flown out together.

46

He didn't have to score every time, Jesse reminded himself. After a couple of quick baskets, he'd take the bounce pass in the high post, wait a few seconds for the defence to collapse around him—elbows in his ribs, outstretched fingers in his eyes—and—ice cool—hit the cutting guard with a no-look back pass—perfectly timed—for an easy lay-up and two points. Coach Higgins had always said he wanted unselfish play— like passing on the letter from Mom to Dad? Jesse didn't think he wanted to know the score there, but it might be a good strategy to pass the ball a lot to impress the new coach, who might even make him a starter.

Adam looked again at the road atlas with the line of connecting roads they had travelled traced up to Billings (by Jesse, with a thick red marker pen). Just across a staple on the facing page, there, only a few minutes away (normally), west along Highway 90 was a tiny blank square outlined in black for Big Timber. Billings to Cutbank, or Sweetgrass, say, on the border, would be 309, plus 5, 314, plus 10 is 324, plus 6 equals 330, plus another 5 is 335, plus 8 from Sunburst to Sweetgrass makes 343 miles, minus the 100, approximately, that they had already driven from Billings, so: 243 miles, about three and a half hours on the road (normally) to reach Canada. Adam remembered his son's excited, romantic talk of camping in the Rockies tomorrow night. And his own dumb romantic decision not to bring a cellular phone. "It will be just the two of us, riding through South Dakota like in *Dances with Wolves*," Adam had told Diane. Yesterday they had camped in those hills black with pine trees where the movie's final slaughter had occurred. Jesse's face was smudged with the day's heat (his hair matted and shooting out at strange angles from pressing against the sun-roof). They were not like Kevin Costner in *Dances with Wolves* who rode through the dust of prairie winds immaculately groomed, with shining skin. After two unwashed days inside, his son's face was gritty and sweaty and scared.

Jesse *loathed* riding the bench.

Adam suddenly felt he was an incompetent father because he knew next to nothing about auto mechanics. And now they were caught in the middle of this hissing ice storm. He had looked for adventure, had wished to drive through another country (and pay $15 U.S. instead of $30 Canadian to fill up the Rabbit's gas tank), had wanted to get away from cities (but had ended up following the industrial interstate to make time, driving through Cleveland, trying to skirt Chicago), and had longed for natural beauty (not fields made uniformly green by giant aluminium sprinklers hooped twenty feet high for rolling which bombarded the sky with mega-gallons). Nothing like this flooding. But at least the hail-stones had stopped battering them. The one wrong turn on the trip (so far) had taken them along a dirt road, next to a tree-lined field where an Amish farmer in a black coat was riding on a cart with two wooden wheels behind two huge-haunched horses, his back to the six-lane highway Adam and Jesse had steered back on. They could survive (if a truck out of nowhere didn't crush them); they had sleeping bags, food, juice, flashlights, some candles for warmth. Adam closed the map book and put it away, knocking the Custer brochure to the floor. That was the only time the Indians had won (except for Oka). "Soldiers drop, and horses fall on them," he read. The engine would start again. "The trend's your friend," were his words of encouragement to his doubtful clients.

Jesse was determined to become a starter—whatever it would take. But he hated screwing up. Coach Higgins' face looking like a purple fist. He couldn't imagine Higgins ever shouting at his father—they were too alike: "Day-dreaming is for losers." Which one had said that? Sometimes Jesse hated the way his dad was always alert—always positive—but that was useful. The ice was changing to rain. He would play confident and smart, and aggressive, so there would be no public put-downs: "It's a defensive rebound. Box out!" If a big guy didn't play tough, he seemed lazy. Forget the cute jumper. If the lane even opened up even a bit, he would *knife* through and dunk hard, and set the picks hard, even in practice. He wouldn't be a wimp. Forget the pain and get off on the check's stunned whoosh of breath as he slammed blindly into you. Outside, the heavy rain was totally drilling them. Most of the fans shouting and high-fiving in the stands wouldn't even know that he had set up the basket as a teammate curled around him for an easy two on the score-sheet, but everyone down on the floor would know his body had made that score happen. In that last game, when Coach Higgins had finally sent him in (only after it had been lost), Jesse's rock-solid pick had crumpled a guy in a red shirt, and, at the end of the game, no one from the other team had dissed him as a clumsy loser.

Adam was worried he might be too old to start again, to manage asset acquisition by eager young brokers, to goose up the firm's profitability, to make a killing in a new province: *Je me souviens*. The road, a twisted red cord stretching all the way back to Montréal, *La*

Belle Province, or *pays*, or *nation*. Beautiful, yes. They had loved the lakes of the Eastern Townships (Was Okanagan going to be like Memphremagog?), the rocky coastline of the Gaspé, old touristy Québec City (where once he had furtively tossed Jesse's shitty diapers into a trash can), but they had never got to the Magdalen Islands (which were supposed to be beautiful). Once, camping in the Laurentians, Diane had jutted her pale, soft-sculpted ass out into the cool piney air, peeing (tickled by a seedling maybe?), but shimmying for him: *belle*. This morning when Adam had wakened with an erection, it felt like he had been sleeping on a tripod.

Jesse tried to forget the envelope. He would forget the showy stutter-step, and even putting the ball on the floor. He was too tall to dribble. By the time the ball had bounced back up to his hand, a small quick guard would have swiped it, and he would look bad in front of the whole school. Forget the sky hook too. No, he'd work on it—but scrap the left-handed version he was too chicken to try in a game anyway. No, he'd practise it. It wasn't useless from in close to the backboard. He'd stay positive, and log the necessary hours—the way Dad did on the phone—to make it happen. It was starting to clear a bit. Jesse would play like he had hair on his ass.

Adam wondered if "montana" was Spanish for "*montagne*" and "mountain." He remembered going fishing with his father, driving over hills on washboard roads in the light-blue Chevy in the dark of morning. His father had been the only one who had ever enjoyed his tuneless singing. Jesse had never pretended (he used to squirm through his lullaby). At the lake Adam's father would slide the boat off the roof of the

Chevy by himself as he stood and watched (so small then). Once, the boat's metal bow had scraped some blue paint from the back of the Chevy, and the raging curses of Adam's father had been terrifying.

The water was icy, but his father would row them out (in steady, measured strokes) to the very middle of the lake while Adam let out his line, with the red and white wavy stripes of the metal lure turning in the clear water. He was sure that the fish could see the dangerous triple hook whose sharp barbs his soft fingertips feared. In that watery place, equidistant from any shore (it seemed), Adam would take over the oars, rowing less expertly, pulling first way to one side, then overcompensating, to the other—in wild spurts and in exhausted drifting—trying again (manfully), only to have an oar swipe loose and spray his father in the stern seat with a shower of lake water. Adam's father would take over again, and row (smoothly) for an hour, during which time they usually caught nothing (not even a nibble), but sometimes to break the boredom Adam would yank back on his rod so suddenly that the line *zinged* out—jerking crazily—pretending he had hooked a whopper (hoping to please his father?). They would head back in for lunch (still trolling), until the boat ran aground. Adam, and then his father, would leap out onto the shore for lunch: sandwiches with thick banana slices on top of peanut butter and hottish Nestle's chocolate out of the red plastic top to the Thermos. Afterwards, his father would take out what he called his "stogie," and would puff away in his unbuttoned coat with the sun shining off his forehead.

Once, Adam's father had said, "Go try casting a few where the river comes in." Adam picked up his big rod, walked away along the lakeshore path, stepping underneath whippy branches, over roots and damp logs, with the gravelly noise getting stronger, until he saw the water burble white. Adam immediately cast his Spin-O-King into a far pool and felt the fierce tug of what he believed to be the rapids—until silver flashed above the river. Suddenly, he realized he had never caught a fish without his father to free its mouth from the triple barbs. He tried to call over the noise of the rapids. But he kept winding the small black handle on the reel—not too fast—and could see the fish coming closer. At the shore it jumped away, and he jerked the rod back, only now remembering to keep the tip up. Adam smoothly wound the fish near once more, lifted it out of the water, and swung its wet silver life over the high grass, and flopped it down by an evergreen tree.

The gills panted so far open, it looked as if a knife had slashed deeply, almost severing the head. Adam dropped the rod and bent down, just as the fish suddenly flipped itself over. It was too close to the water, so he had to pick up the slippery, slimy thing and throw it farther onto land so it couldn't get away (though it was still attached to the line). Adam had forgotten to dip his hand in the water first as his father had taught him (so the scales wouldn't come off and the fish could live if he had to toss it back for being too small). But this one was very big, at least the length of a ruler, and it lay inert. Adam leaned forward to look at the dead fish, and, all at once, it wrenched over, and he jumped back. Embarrassed at being a scaredy cat (a sissy), Adam searched for a club, like the one in the boat, but here there were only branches on trees. He broke part of one off, and began hitting the frantic fish. But the stick was small and pliable and pretty useless, and the fish just kept flopping, covering itself in bits of leaves and dirt, its gill gashes opening and closing like crazy, its eyes staring back at him. But at last, it lay really dead.

Adam took a deep breath, and picked it up by its thin vee-shaped tail. And the fish twisted free of his fingers! Hollow inside, he grabbed it and whammed it against the trunk of a tree, but the fish (now somehow off the hook) shot out of his hand, ending up in a berry bush, a foot off the ground, as if it were trying to swim through the air, back to the river. Trembling, Adam took it in both hands—one of its eyes hanging half out—squeezed tight, and stumbled towards the water, nearly tripping over the rod, and heaved it into the middle of the fast-running river. It was swept away, floating on its back, towards the lake. Adam felt hot tears run down his cheeks. When he tried to wash his hands in the cold river, silver scales stuck to his wet sleeve. He walked back to the rod, stuck one of the triple barbs into the long soft cork handle and wound the line up so tight the fibreglass rod bowed, just as if there had been a big fish on the end.

Jesse could see phantom lights slowly coming at them. It might as well be now that he broke the news (whatever) to his father. Jesse hated keeping it any longer—had patiently waited for the right moment, but who could tell? Timing was everything—taking that explosive first step past the defender. A station wagon with its roof-rack full, going the other way in a blur, threw off water like geysers from its turning wheels—splatting their stopped Rabbit. His father had never cried in front of him. ("Don't drag your pivot foot.")

53

Jesse swiveled, still watching his father's eyes, feeling in back for his gym bag. Actually, if Jesse had to be stuck in a car through the cold night with someone, it might as well have been with his father—his hard skull shape with the stupid hat off looked undefeatable. ("Don't try to look good out there. Win!" Coach Higgins had said.) He unzipped the bag, found the jacket pocket, and pulled out the envelope.

When Adam had walked back around to where his father was waiting (hands on hips), he had been asked, "Any luck, Tookie?" (Why hadn't he ever given Jesse a nickname?) Adam had then told him about the fish he had landed and how he had thrown it back into the river. His father had patted his son's crew-cut head and had said there was a good chance such a tough fish would survive and they could tell Adam's mother they hadn't been skunked. Adam had wanted to go home then, but his father said that would be silly. Later, on the long drive back, Adam had refused to sing.

Jesse thought his dad must have fallen asleep—his body was slumped and still—but, no, he could see both his eyes were open, staring straight at the windshield. Jesse rested the letter on the steering wheel. He, too, was a thousand miles away, but in which direction?

Adam pictured the collection of small metal boxes with their numbers (like grey mailboxes). One, part-way up and to the right, held his father's ashes.

Jesse was eager to get going. Rotating his head clockwise, then counter-clockwise, to relax his neck, he picked the letter off the steering wheel (which was smaller in diameter than a hoop) and held it out to his father: "Mom asked me to give you this when we reached the Rockies."

Adam took the envelope in both hands. It was clear enough to see now. Diane's underlining of his name looked ominous, like an accountant's bottom line (her soft-sculpted ass). Adam loved Jesse for the gentleness in his voice. He had her dark brown eyes, her big teeth, her thin nose (but was *his* son). All at once, Adam wanted to go fishing with Jesse, to leave debentures and derivatives behind, to go Indian. This was not a late valentine.

Jesse glanced at his father, who kept the letter moving—rotating it—holding a new corner of the rectangle each time pinched between his thumb and index finger, shifting it from one hand to the other, like a cross-over dribble.

Adam felt clogged by paper—this envelope, the Visa gas bills (shiny paper that was too oily and transparent to feel like paper) littering the floor, campsite receipts of small stiff green cardboard, the glossy Custer brochure (which had fallen again), the inky dated passes to national parks, the bulky road atlas (its cover almost ripped right off, and its insides torn in all the places they had been). The landscape of Wyoming had looked like a motion picture, a backdrop for a Western. The Badlands. ("Are you in love with someone else?" "Christ, I'm not even in love with myself," Diane had answered.) That time in the lodge after cross-country skiing, when Adam had happened upon Luc and her, his chubby little hand massaging her stiff back under her blouse, a black bra strap hanging down her left ribs—the innocent bitch (*belle*)!

Jesse twisted the key and the engine started, first time, with Lyle Lovett bursting out loudly with "Further Down the Line" before he could turn the radio off. A line of traffic passed them, heading west.

Adam was scared their Montréal life together would be shredded if he tore open this envelope. Delay it a bit longer. With all this litter, he and Jesse had been carrying their own world in here (for miles and miles). Placing the envelope on his lap, Adam fluttered back the pages of the atlas. A red umbilical cord tied them to Montréal, which pulsed with life between the river and the mountains (*Les Canadiens sont là!*). And it was O.K. that Jesse hadn't wanted to play hockey; basketball had kept him in school. Now his son was waiting to drive off, his neck relaxed against the driver's headrest. The map of Montréal, Adam thought, looked like what he imagined a placenta to be: a bloody mess with a red line extending outward. Like a heart, it had a solid mass: afterbirth—his son—the twisted cord holding us together—discarded. It was confusing. One time, imitating Luc's pronunciation, Diane had said, "Truss me." Her white stretch marks had nourished their six-foot five-inch son Jesse. Adam could sense the almost weightless envelope on his shorts. He was grateful to be a passenger for awhile and had this weird wish to see a living placenta.

Jesse rolled his window all the way down and stuck his head out backwards into the light slanting rain.

Adam scrunched the atlas into the door compartment, breathed deeply, and said, "O.K., Big Timber, hit it."

Accelerating smoothly, Jesse pulled back out onto the freeway.

The
Malcolm Lowry
Professional Development
Grant

As soon as the cockpit door opens (*aeropuerto*), your throat will begin to ache. You will remember having heard that breathing the air of Mexico City is the equivalent of smoking two packs a day. You will want to say to the not-so-tall but dark and handsome stranger (despite those pock-marks), "*Gracias, pero estoy ocupada,*" but because you will not be sure of your Berlitz Spanish, the first of your potential Latin lovers will hear: "Thank you, but I'm busy." Walking down the aisle with your carry-on bag, you will touch the girdle-like money belt around your waist that holds your passport (*pasaporte*), American bills, paper pesos, and even your traveller's cheques.

A smiling, grey-haired man will take your visa, and

you will be feeling for the Mexican coins for tipping that you will have secreted in the inner pocket of your linen jacket in Los Angeles, when you realize that somehow you have stepped out in front of a machine gun (a word not included in your Berlitz travel guide). You will have joined a line of people moving unfazed past the hyper-alert eyes of a young soldier guarding a bank. You will wonder why you didn't just go to Hawaii.

Your taxi will be a cute pastel green-and-cream beetle. The driver will zoom off, looking for any hint of an opening—right or left—to dart into, and speed along the broad highway with the VW hood centred exactly on a white lane line. First men, then packs of kids, and finally grandmothers, will run out in front of your hurtling taxi. Lurching like suicidal matadors, they will cross between buildings of warm pink, bleached purple, dingy and acrid yellow, and different shades of jungle green. Not once will your driver slow, or swerve, and you will remember horror stories and realize that you don't know what to do *when* he kills someone. Desperately, you will want to tell him to stop this macho stupidity, but the only Spanish phrase that will pop into your brain is ¡*Al ladron!* and you will fear that your command "Stop thief!" will enrage him to a sure act of vehicular homicide, which now will be your fault. After only ten minutes in Mexico, you will find yourself wondering how many thousands of pesos it will take to bribe yourself free after the fatal accident and get back to the *aeropuerto*, and Canada. Your Berlitz Guide will have a chart in back for tipping porters, waiters, maids, hairdressers, and lavatory attendants, but no useful suggestions about *policia* or judges.

But soon your taxi will be spinning you around

the huge *zocalo*—and the square's endless flatness will seem unreal in this gorgeous clutter of a city. One-way traffic will enclose your whining beetle as it rushes past the windowed symmetry of the stone palace, past the green metal scaffolding stretching up the high, impossibly ornate cathedral, and, when your driver brakes suddenly, you will cringe—look over your shoulder for the expected crash—but *nada*, and on stepping out, you will find there isn't a scratch on the VW's two-tone painted shell. Though your eyes will be stinging from the harsh air, you will be so glad to be standing alive and unhurt by the entrance to the Gran Hotel Ciudad de Mexico, and the money in your hand will look so strangely blue that you will pay the driver with *poco* anxiety about being cheated. At the hotel doorway, however, you will flinch when the little girl with a smudged face and a little crutch bumps into you with one hand out, "*Señorita, por favor,*" and you will be *mucho* relieved to get inside the chandeliered lobby with its iron-caged elevators and hanging papier-mâché *piñatas*—red and spiky and festive and bulbous with the promise of gifts and candies.

Dr. Sachs walked across the *zocalo* (officially known as the Plaza de la Constitucion), and entered the middle gate of the fortress-like Palacio Nacional de Mexico. Above the staircase a man with a metal jacket had his knee between the legs of an Indian woman who had been forced on her back. And beside a cauldron (like a kettle drum glowing orange) three men were branding a trussed-up brown human body. A two-legged beast with a jaguar skin, blood-red lips, and sharp white incisors lanced a falling Conquistadore in the back. There in the mural's centre was the founding prophecy of the Aztecs, an eagle on a cactus holding an orange multiheaded snake in its mouth. Dr. Sachs felt more bewildered than exhilarated.

The lighting, both clear (*claro*) and shadowy (*oscuro*), bounced differently off the grand composite images framed beneath the seven deep, adjoining archways that folded in and out like a massive, half-defective accordion. There was also little accord between Dr. Sachs's expectations of Diego Rivera's art and this sombre, brilliant clutter of peopled violence. Neither the stone and marble architecture nor the brain's oxymorons (crude subtlety? lyrical Stalinism?) could contain the energies of these pulsating forms that were at once drab and garish. *Secuencia de la historia de Mexico*. But there was no evident *sequence* in these seven huge jumbled pictorial segments flowing and flaming and breathing into one incoherent panorama, only an intense feeling that the past must have been lived like the present: "confused, multiform, and unintelligible" (in the words of Paul Ricoeur).

The far *left* panel (that turned a corner) had Karl Marx in Heaven—the dead white European male painted above everyone else—leaning on a brick factory chimney of industrialization, a sun ringed orange-red dawning at his back, his arm outstretched and his index finger pointing, telling the Mexicans what to do with history, and offering the viewer a doubly consoling plot: narrative order and human triumph through class struggle. This story line would now displease environmentalists, feminists, "communists" who had ripped apart the Berlin Wall, and the intellectually decolonizing thinkers of South America. Could Diego

Rivera, once friend of the soon-to-be-assassinated Trotsky, have been so willfully naive as to paint ideological clarity into the unintelligible shadows of human experience?

On the opposite wall, the pre-Conquest alternative, the legend of Quetzalcoatl. His truncated, upside-down sun-face did not notice the tax collector below, or even the strange flying beast with two fiery tongues hovering above the molten lava of an exploding volcano. Staring at the inverted eyes of the pre-Hispanic sun god, Dr. Sachs's own eyes began to water and hurt.

Visiting time was over. But Dr. Sachs kept looking at Rivera's unsettling depiction of Mexico's national emblem. It made iconographic sense that the snake was the same orange as the Quetzalcoatl sun, the erupting volcano, the fiery cannon of the Conquistadores, the monks burning the codices, but why was there, near one end of the snake, a circling band from which four cloth-like cones terminated in four bright miniature balls? Dr. Sachs knew better, but rubbed at irritated eyes. The snake's head, multibelled in appearance, looked like the cap of a court-jester. Mexican life, a joke?

After re-reading my mother's letter (Lucy, they're out there. You're just not looking!) I stare up at the dining room's elegant ceiling and want to take a stick to the fat red *piñata* hanging over my head. (Your second cousin Sam's new bride, Jessica, wanted to sing at her own wedding—"Stairway to Heaven"— but had a fit and threw her diamond ring at Uncle Max when he suggested the lyrics might be prophetic, given Sam's problems with his new pace-maker.)

By myself at dinner I feel the ache of the blues.

This beer, with its two big red Xs, doesn't improve my mood. Maybe it's because I've got the two Xs of the female chromosome, Dos Equis, or maybe it's because I told the shy waiter *claro* instead of *oscuro*, and now this light-coloured liquid makes me see too clearly. (Get down on your knees and thank your lucky stars you didn't marry David who just got out of detox for the ceremony and was caught with his hand inside Aunt Eva's purse. First he said he was only looking for some Kleenex; then he claimed he was trying to find some Tums for the butterflies that always start flying around in his stomach whenever he shows up at a wedding, and finally he told Aunt Eva he wanted to borrow her vibrator! By this time his poor mother was crying her heart out, her face a black river of mascara . . .)

"*Señora?*"

"*Oui . . . oui*, I mean, *si, si.*" My brain tries to accommodate via the more familiar strangeness of French. "*Otra cerveza.* Dos Equis. *Oscuro. Oscuro.*" I wonder if he went to the wedding hoping to see me—this maudlin blob in a red dress in a foreign country.

My mother thinks I should smash my way to happiness—just blindfold myself, grab a long stick, and whack at what I hope is the *piñata's* belly until the sweets of the world tumble down onto my lap.

David's sweet soprano sax I remember once, on a hot New York night, trembling with the sounds of love (maybe).

"*Gracias.*"

You will panic when the commercial jet (*Servicio Azteca de oro*) tilts suddenly towards the snowy peak just outside your window. When the plane immediately rights itself, you will relax, realizing that the pilot—like a barnstormer from an old newsreel—has just tipped his wings to Mount Popocatepetl.

Later, bouncing on the runway at the Puerto Escondido *aeropuerto*, someone will say, "It's only eighty degrees," and you will be happy to be a long way from Ottawa and winter.

And at the hotel, Flor de Maria, with its white hand-plastered walls, the cement floor gouged and blackened to look like huge tiles, and fiesta colours everywhere, you will feel a sense of exotic exuberance, especially looking out from room *número quince* (**keen**say), at roosters, cabanas, palm and banana trees, and *el mar*.

At the sea's ragged edge, you will wade warmly. Then, lying on your new beach towel, you will watch three brown boys scoop up small fish trapped by the turning tide and then hand cast lines with this living bait to pull in larger fish (*pescado*). Pelicans, whose mouths are not so pouchy here, will glide above the glassy sliding crests, waiting, like the crouching blonde surfer with a black knee-bandage, for the right wave. A woman in a shimmering dress will offer you one of the twenty hammocks bowing down her back, and you will say, "N*ada . . . gracias . . . nada.*"

In the humid room Dr. Sachs took out a spiral notebook, disorderly scraps of paper, and tiny pallid postcards. If events were threaded by time, then Diego Rivera had cut the warp strings—had pulled the rug out from underneath history. (A)voiding chronology, he was both the monarch of all he surveyed *and* the king's mocking court-jester. But the problem with seeing history as a joke was that it wasn't very funny. Also, for a punch line to work, the joke needed a sequence. Did the religious zeal of the monks burning the codices (*naranja*) come before, with, or after the cannon fire (*naranja*) of the Spanish soldiers, and where did nature, the exploding (*naranja*) volcano fit? All those orange images in the mural must be trying to make history intelligible.

How was Dr. Sachs going to produce a paper on Malcolm Lowry, Diego Rivera, and narrativity that would justify the travel grant?

I look at a mother and daughter walking barefoot towards me on this scorching sand, each with a wide straw basket full of sandals on their heads. For the bulky mother the burden seems automatic, unfelt, but the (seven-year-old?) girl needs to keep reaching up to hold this weight in place.

I can barely imagine the skills needed to craft the beautifully stitched tan leatherwork taken down from their heads. Pointing to my pink feet, to the moulded air-pocketed sandals whose raised purple letters spell "Nike," I again say, "*Nada.*"

I hate to watch the brown-eyed *niña* lift her basket up towards the sun, see her fighting to get the balance right on that small, rounded skull, while her mother sticks the huge basket back up top as if on a spike and observes her daughter's efforts—wobble, slip, grab, not holding on now—just as Ma did when I was learning to skate backwards on the frozen canal.

You will be sitting near the pool, on the rooftop deck of the Flor de Maria, gazing at *el mar azul*, sipping your

64

glass of chilled white wine, believing you must be the only tourist in Mexico who needs a laxative, when you will hear a rustling above you in the vines and open rafters. Up in the corner, sitting on a thin plywood board, is a largish *gato* with black patches on tawny fur and big, darkly luminous eyes, and you will say, *"Buenas tardes"* to the owner's pet ocelot, and feel contented.

Dr. Sachs unfolded the small poster of the mural. *If* the Aztec myth of the founding of their empire was painted into the very centre of the middle panel by Rivera, and the depiction of the class struggle (relegated to a side wall) separated from the eagle on a cactus eating a snake by many intervening, magnificently vivid, but collectively incoherent images, *then* the Marxist narrative itself, instead of foreclosing through teleological revolution the heterogeneity of history, might be exposed ironically as historicized fantasy.

Refolding *Secuencia de la historia de Mexico*, Dr. Sachs picked up the Penguin edition of Malcolm Lowry's *Under the Volcano*, with its cover illustration taken from Rivera's fresco, *Day of the Dead in the City*, itself centred on a man downing a glass—his eyes pressed shut.

Waking to pee, I get an unexpected gift: the delicate pink light of dawn over fluttering palm leaves. Looking from the narrow bathroom window at the ruffled sea, I remember our family visiting David and his mother one spring, and his gift of cut branches. I was expecting all the buds to come out as pink blossoms. I still can't forgive my mother for the telling, and retelling, of his gesture as "the terminal dumbness of Lucy's first boyfriend." Now I would be far from disappointed to see a bouquet of buds come out as new green leaves.

The sun is turning the rose sky blankly white.

You will stroll along the beach to the curve where *los pescadores* gun their boats up onto the sand above the tideline, where eager women with knives lift out and gut the silver fish. You will walk on, towards the rocks and the lighthouse, following a stone path, past the initials of lovers scratched into circular cactus pods, over foot-bridges crafted from cement, and will be startled at the scuttle of a huge iguana.

Returning for breakfast, you will hear pinging, as *los pescadores* hammer at rudders and propellers, straightening and fixing, while the women tie new knots in the drying nets. You will think you detect a cheeping noise from sand-coloured crabs chased by running shore birds.

At the table, to the polite, baffled waitress, you will keep saying, "*Oui . . . oui.*" The bananas, small and newly picked, will loll deliciously on your tongue, sweeten your breathing.

Spinning the pages of the novel, Dr. Sachs read:

The flare lit up the whole *cantina* with a burst of brilliance in which the figures at the bar—that he now saw included besides the little children and the peasants who were quince or cactus farmers in loose white clothes and wide hats, several women in mourning from the cemeteries and dark-faced men in dark suits

66

with open collars and their ties undone—appeared, for an instant, frozen, a mural. . . .

Dr. Sachs knew critics had interpreted *Under the Volcano* ("backwards revolved the luminous wheel" at the foot of this page) in terms of cinema and Buddhism, but was this passage at the end of the opening chapter, and, more specifically, the word, "mural," a kind of *mise-en-abyme*, a miniature inner mirror to the novel's artistry? And was this putting into the abyss of endlessly reflecting mirrors related to Lowry's *barranca*, the ravine into which the hero's corpse is thrown on the last page? But the beach was not a place for intellect, or ethics.

Carleton University would not be pleased, Dr. Sachs suspected, to learn that most of the funded research time had been spent at the resort village of Puerto Escondido. What plausible narrative could be constructed?

(Lucy, they're out there.) I should send Ma a postcard in Hawaii, but the sun's too hot. A siesta?

She has a sense of humour for everyone else: Why not for me? At that first post-marriage party she gave, with Larry, my new, roly-poly stepfather, she must have sat on the floral sofa for three hours with a string of film negatives looped around her neck, her face expectant, amused. Wearing an Expos cap, he scratched at his crotch, and laughed like a burro.

No one could guess: Some day my prince will come.

I'm too tired to write.

At the neighbouring Hotel Santa Fe you will eat garlic red snapper with *media botella de vino blanco*, will say

67

"*Muy bien, gracias,*" and will wonder if you saw this headless *pescado* flopping on the bottom of a beached boat in the morning. Also, for a flickering moment, you will ask yourself why those seated have light skins while those carrying things have darker pigmentation, but you will remind yourself you're here on vacation— to have a good time—and the sunset will fill the warm Pacific sky with at least an hour of postcard colour.

And, after, you will decide to tell the tall, red-haired Australian, "*No, no me unteresa, gracias,*" and not worry about the Spanish pronunciation marks you can never remember, but will feel cruel having to translate for him, "I'm not interested, thank you."

Returning along the beach, you will be listening to *el mar* and watching the light of *la luna* on the wave-tips, when a short man will hold a bright knife with a rusty edge in your face. You will give him all the paper pesos and confusing coins in your pocket *rapidamente*, and will get back to the hotel *rapidamente*.

Unable to sleep, Dr. Sachs found the light switch in the dark, sat up in bed, and flipped through the pages of the spiral notebook. There was the quote from Paul Ricoeur about "the undeniable asymmetry between the referential modes of historical and fictional narrative." But the problem was that the same word(s) and image(s) had to be used for both what had happened and what had been made up. Before Rivera painted his murals, horrible things like colonialism had *happened*, but *as* representation this knowledge entered a zone of mere "meaning," cohabiting with the fictive, or even with hate-mongering fantasy like the *Protocols of the Elders of Zion*.

If there was no way to tell apart the telling of fiction from the telling of history, then the knife held to the throat might as well be made out of paper.

I can't say, "The weather is here, wish you were beautiful."

I can't forget to put the "Dear" in front of "Ma." This date, "Dec. 22," seems fraught with soft heaviness for me, like the postcard's image of Rivera's *Flower Day*, an enormous basket of cut white blossoms.

> *I guess there are no adventures without misadventures. Sometimes Mexico has the feel of a big family wedding gone wrong, but no one wanted it to end up that way, so, along with the harshness, there's a forgiving warmth. Say "Hi" to the "Prince" for me. Lucy*

The man with tight pants, spare gestures, and pale sunglasses who takes your ticket for the chartered flight will turn out to be the pilot of this twin-propped plane (no co-pilot), and as you are flying out over *el mar* as a way of gaining height before taking on the inland mountains, you will wonder if there is anyone in the control tower. Your ears will ache in the (unpressurized?) cabin, and you will be very scared at the way he is steering—just above the jungle ravines and *between* the mountain peaks which disappear into clouds.

Dr. Sachs re-read the echoing sentence, starting midway, trying to separate it from personal associations:

(. . . to persuade herself her journey was neither thoughtless nor precipitate, and on the plane when she knew it was both, that she should have warned him, that it was abominably unfair to take him by surprise.)

Skipping further down the page, searching for the word "Oaxaca," Dr. Sachs found where last night's re-reading of *Under the Volcano* had stopped:

The word was like a breaking heart, a sudden peal of stifled bells in a gale, the last syllables of one dying of thirst in the desert. Did she remember Oaxaca! The roses and the great tree, was that, the dust and the buses to Etla and Nochitlán? and: "*damas acompañadas de un caballero, gratis!*" Or at night their cries of love, rising into the ancient fragrant Mayan air, heard only by ghosts?

Dr. Sachs was half-puzzled by Lowry's language of elegiacal desire for a place where he had been thrown in jail for debts and drunkenness, and pondered if Lowry's prose here had become "sentimentalized" by internal focalization through the female character of Yvonne, and if this were a psycholinguistic gender stereotyping, or perhaps had its source(s) in the biographies of Lowry's first and second wives (whose emotional expressiveness likely had been previously (de)formed through hegemonic social construction). Dr. Sachs also questioned the vague reference to "Mayan air," since Mayans didn't live anywhere near Oaxaca. Additionally, Dr. Sachs wondered why it was impossible to enjoy reading a book anymore.

I'm tired, and the cigar smoke is getting to me, but two wonderful musicians, Gil and Cartas, are playing on the violin and guitar in this roofed-over courtyard, El

Sol y La Luna. I'm thinking about my hotel bed at the Parador Plaza, just across the street (*calle*), when I recognize the first bars of "Djangology."

Felipe Moreno enters with an *amigo*, waves to me. Earlier, I talked to him at the contemporary *museo* about his weavings that had alternating patterns made by sewing strips of cloth over the wool before dying, then unstitching them to emphasize the bands of complete blankness among the colours (except where the needle's piercings left dots of dye). He had suggested El Sol y La Luna for *la musica*.

As I clap for Gil and Cartas, Felipe comes over to my table, alone, wearing a silk shirt. I gesture towards the empty chair, and the musicians begin to play a fast dance. I order two Dos Equis, *claro*, and Felipe insists on paying for both drinks.

La musica begins to fill my head with the dizzying light of both the sun and the moon.

It's not *claro* at what point I have decided not to use the phrase that starts with an upside-down exclamation mark, ¡*Dejeme tranquila, por favor*! because I already know I don't want to be left alone.

At the Oaxaca runway, although you were first in line, the pilot will board the heavy German couple and two male passengers before you, up front, to balance the helter-skelter stacking of bulging cardboard boxes in back where you will sit.

For ten minutes you will hear the twin engines run roughly without the left propeller going around, and then you will see the pilot step down out of the tiny cockpit, spin the immobile prop once by hand, and climb back in.

As the overloaded plane lunges forward and eventually stumbles off the runway's end into the shimmering afternoon sky, you will feel an odd fatalism, and nod off.

Standing again in front of *Secuencia de la historia de Mexico* with its populist cartoon boldness, Dr. Sachs wondered some more about Rivera's wife, who had once been occluded, but had recently become a feminist cult figure. Dr. Sachs walked down the corridor to look for a second time at the husband's ambiguous representation of Frida Kahlo, the most prominent figure in his depiction of Mexico's Aztec origins—lifting her dress to expose one knee, her chin up. Was Frida Kahlo's own small-scale art and obsessive self-portraiture a necessary refusal and narcissistic strategy of survival under the masterful, monumental male gaze?

Or did Lowry have it right (at least, textually), *"No se puede vivir sin amar,"* and the super-subtle critic had no useful analytic vocabulary (voyeurism? hierarchization?) for understanding that Diego simply wanted to paint Frida, the woman he loved to live with, as the beginning of everything? In fact, Dr. Sachs wondered if the shift in Rivera's master narrative from Marxism to Catholicism made public during his final illness could be traced to Frida's earlier death.

Rivera's dark and bright mural bits, Dr. Sachs sensed through stinging eyes, had to be understood as discrete parts implying the wish for a completed and intelligible whole, a way of making tangible the human fragments that are the open-ended hurt of history.

I am riding in a taxi through this city that's nearly as

populous as my own country, and at Alameda Square it seems all the people in Mexico City have gathered. In lines blocks long, families wait for the seated red-coated figure on a raised platform in the park. The taxi halts in the middle of brown faces shining in the sun, and neatly dressed bodies cross over into the park, and I see another red-coated figure further down the long park, with its own enormous gathering, and yet another, further away and smaller, and still another, in a near infinite mirroring. Along the full length of Alameda Square there must be at least two dozen Santas!

And I think of David that Christmas time in New York, hopping down from the bandstand at the break, strolling over to the bar, asking me why Santa had no kids. Thinking that this was a different David, I was shaking my head even as he said, "He always comes down chimneys." Why did it sound more brutal than hip?

During that final set his saxophone collected every last sixteenth note and muted half-rhythm from the other musicians in the quintet, and he put everything into one long solo that sang, honked, and soared, screeched and whispered and wailed, and sang again, but felt nothing like his gift to me of leafy summer abundance, just six months earlier. David's last solo seemed too self-regarding, aggrandizing, maybe only a magnificent performance of self, but what else is a *solo*?

And when I went to visit him in that cramped dressing room five minutes after the show, he just grabbed me under my sweater, under my bra, roughly squeezing my breast like it was a *piñata* to break open. "Not like this," I said. And he let go, his coked-up eyes wandering back to the beautiful tubular curve of his instrument lying diagonally on a chair.

73

This taxi won't get me to the *aeropuerto* in time for the flight.

Why should I want to send him a postcard?

> *December 24.*
> *Dear David, I've been hanging out at the beach, trying to relate Malcolm Lowry's narrative structure to Diego Rivera's murals, but thinking how it's like melodic lines in jazz, something to jump free from, or like fishermen's nets just tied together to make openings. I never thanked you for those branches of budded leaves. To quote Malcolm Lowry, "No se puede vivir sin amar," meaning, "I-you-one can't live without love."*
> Gracias.
> *Lucy.*

This taxi's going nowhere. ¿So? ¿What self-imposed narrative plots my return to a cold grey city of colourless skins?

At Los Angeles you will have your passport taken as if it belongs to someone else. (You'll never make anything of yourself unless you go to collage.) Your identity will be read aloud, "Dr. Lucy Sachs," while his eyes fix on your face, before moving down to the official sameness, the photo that glints under the fluorescent lights, like a broken, half-dark blade.

You will be given back your picture, upside down.

With her name, in my hand.

Holding on.

74

Convection

You wake up to find a vowel on your leg.

It's just above the right knee, nestled in some dark hairs. A small brown mole that seems familiar is to its left, and a hard white fleck that you sort of recall is just above the vowel that has never been there before. You're positive it wasn't there last night when you came home to the dark apartment—after she had said you were through.

But you weren't looking for a vowel then, or now. Hiding and not hiding, it is maybe an inch and a half from the curved sheen of the *patella*, with its stringy football scar. You can barely remember being straightened up at the line of scrimmage—before a diving linebacker with a fat letter "S" on his helmet smashed you sideways. But this is not about consonants. It is a vowel sticking to your skin!

Near where the leg bends. You quite can't see it—somehow you just *feel* it, on top of several thin horizontal patches of skin cells. Or is it right *inside* your flesh?

Maybe you can't make out its form because it's buried below the epidermis, or whatever. What was she trying to tell you last night? Some kind of exchange there, but nothing really tangible—not something you could kick like a pigskin full of air.

This vowel is starting to itch. What about the blood circulation? Should you have left your blue pajamas on? But you didn't know it was there then. Scratch it? It might come off. Isn't that what you *want*? Not with your flesh attached.

What is this vowel doing glued to your leg? You reach your hand down to touch, but it might spread, become an infection of letters. A comma might lodge itself under your fingernail.

Maybe the vowel will simply wash off. Or fall off—tomorrow—like a scab, if left alone. Where do scabs go? As a kid, you couldn't figure out the mystery of their disappearance. Lost in jeans washed in the dryer? Your hand hovers above the vowel, fingers spread wide.

That's how she waved good-bye, slender fingers fanned out—like she was still friendly. She didn't have the guts to . . .

You touch it. Or almost. *Very* close anyway, before the vowel tingled. Scary. The pulses of (imagined?) heat made you jerk your hand back, and now your pink-creviced palm is up beside your face, and you are star-

76

ing at it for damage, or expecting to see maybe a weird apostrophe. But you have no burning sensation, no fingertip redness, no prickling sensation, no evidence your hand touched anything, let alone a *vowel*. Earlier there definitely was something hot, but, now, no sign of any heat transfer.

You're not imagining this, are you? If it had a word shape, maybe, you wouldn't be so confused. You only know a sound has somehow grafted itself down there.

Why had she gotten so mad? Her lips ugly with questions about why you thought you knew what was going on inside her head. Sure is a different brain beneath those springy black curls you loved to feel. Call her. Touch it. Avowal. One word.

Instead, you pick up the pen by the phone. Maybe it's the "uh" sound you are seeing. Your tongue in the middle of your half-open mouth, when you don't know what to say next.

There is nothing really visible on your skin for your eyes to focus on, for your hand to copy onto the yellow phone pad with its pale blue lines. So you read your black pen: "Onyx Faber-Castell Micro" and "Japan." You're getting mixed up. Why are you reading a pen that's supposed to write words for someone else to read? What do you expect when a fucking *vowel* gloms onto your leg in the middle of the night? And you are scared that you might have to carry it around forever because you don't know how it landed there. Might it be a horrible flesh-eating disease?

Tentatively, you direct the pen's hard metal point towards the invisible vowel. The silvery tip of your Onyx pen begins to tremble. You stop, carefully lift the black pen away, and set it down parallel to the phone, all the while keeping both eyes on that vowel thing.

Is there a pink spot now? No. You're just straining your eyes—squinting because you're getting old and you need glasses. And you tell yourself to take a deep breath, which sinks inside of you, coolly, densely.

What did she say—after you had told that joke told to you by that Brian guy, the real estate agent with tasseled shoes, who got it off the Internet, who's pressuring you to complete the duplex evaluation? There are no good comparables for that property. It just looks out of place—next to dark hairs, shiny segments of skin. What have you ever done to a vowel?

"I don't deserve this," she said, not looking at you. There's no itchiness, no discoloration, no lump, *nothing*, just a harmless little vowel. You had retold the story of the guy who got on the elevator with a woman in a fur coat who said to him, "You have fifteen floors to prove to me I'm a woman," so he quickly undid the buttons on his shirt, whipped it off, and said, "Iron this."

Not laughing, she inspected the dust on the ivory venetian blinds, closed against the city, the night. Pretended no sounds had been uttered.

Right now you would like to be able to do that trick of looking off into somewhere else, as if nothing has happened. You stare at the calendar on your bedroom wall, and see snowy landscapes, and read the word, "December," and figure out it's a Monday, and the month's second day, then shift your gaze back, and focus very hard on your hard round hairless knee.

But your peripheral vision tells you that your vowel

(like bad breath) has not gone away. It is not a "none," it is a lurking presence. And you're disturbed at not even knowing *which* vowel it is, hooked into your skin.

Have you forgotten what they are? Maybe it's like when you try to remember a name, and you have to go through the whole alphabet, letter by letter, to find the missing one. Sometimes it works. Try. "A." You're only aware of your foolish voice bouncing off the far wall and back to your anxious ears. Nothing flinched down there. It's time to just get up and go to the doctor's, and have it removed. Simple.

Is the vowel—whichever it is—getting more deeply embedded? Eating now? Don't get paranoid. Easy for you to say. What if Dr. White can't see it? Shut up. He would send you to a shrink.

What time is it? 8:27. It's a Sony! You're supposed to be in the office in thirty-three minutes.

No one would notice the vowel under your pants. You would know it was there. But not visible, not on public show like that large scarlet letter that Puritan woman had to wear around her neck for having sex. Adultery. Usually childish. Your vowel didn't answer, *eh*? "A" is not your scarlet letter. Maybe if you lean your ear towards your right knee—dangerously close— you could *hear* the vowel, squeaking maybe, like a rodent. Was that a faint hum?

Last night, on the floral couch, she interrupted you to say you were always interrupting, and that you always loved to listen to your own voice. She had gone on talking for a long time about not being allowed to talk, and needing to express her needs, and you had been afraid to interrupt as her squeaky high-pitched nasal voice talked on and on—like a sharp curved tool relentlessly scraping off the plaque beneath your soft gums—on and on, with words that weren't hers, but Oprah's, or someone else's, or nobody's, and you could start to predict the decreasing length of intervals between reminders that this was "sharing," and, at last, you knew for certain you would miss the Highlight Show at eleven that would have kept you up-to-date in your hockey pool.

You just take in air and breathe it out again, with sounds attached. All those things like the voice-box (larynx?), and the tongue and teeth and lips. Her black curls like some drunken dream of pubic hair. She gives such great head.

"E!" Your vowel, whichever it is, just lies there, inert. Like you're not exciting enough to get it to respond, to turn it on. So you try everything. "I!" "O!" Last chance. "U!" And sometimes it just doesn't work out. Screw it! It's always the guy's fault.

If that goddamn vowel doesn't get the hell off you *now*, it's in deep shit. You'll rip its puny, invisible, mouthy shape right out of your flesh.

8:38 a.m.

Haven't you been forgetting "and sometimes 'y'"? It can be used as a vowel. "White, bite, height, might." No. "Kind, bind." No. Right now you can't think of any words that use it. "Lined, signed." Anyway, they must exist, those words with "y." Just try it. You shout out: "Y!" Your question must have shoved every particle of air around your room twice, but still the dumb vowel lies there, like a corpse.

Saturday night, two weeks ago, after you both had watched *Pulp Fiction*, she wanted you a lot. Out of her open mouth all those sounds came, kept coming. Her breathing a bellowing out of deep grunts, and all the hot vowels in the world blown past your face, out the window into a night of cold stars. And near the end, you heard an ambulance siren.

But last night, she asked for the silver hexagonal key back.

And now this silent thing with no shape you can make out acting like it's a permanent part of you—like that long-ago scar. At the line of scrimmage.

Why would you call her? 8:49 a.m. You're going to be late. Now you're standing beside your black Ikea bed on the chilled rug—thinking that the ceiling's probably warm. Your hands have automatically snatched up the discarded blue Jockey underpants—freezing—and you step the clenched toes of your left leg through one hole. Pausing, you lift your veined right foot, balance yourself, then knife it through the other hole, before carefully stretching wide the elastic and cotton to slip untouchingly past the sleeping vowel. It doesn't squeak, or anything.

You can walk around fine. But you understand the vowel's waiting—like a squirrel clinging to a tree. Your right leg *feels* O.K. You try hopping a little, over to the chair. You grab the brown pants which need pressing, but which you can wear for one more day. Jerk them on, cover it up, and look in the mirror: you're back to normal.

You'll just get some juice, and forget about the existence of every single vowel you've ever heard.

"Heard, herd." Why are there two ways to spell the same sound? "Bird and turd." Now you have four ways to write one vowel sound! "Words." That makes five ways! And that old folk-rock group, "The Byrds"—and sometimes "y." You gulp down the grapefruit juice, strangely excited.

And depressed. There's no link. No clear one-to-one relationship between sound and sense. She wanted you to "commit." What? Suicide? Murder? Panting in, "uh, uh, uh, uh," and moaning out, the hot air moving freely across her tongue, "oh, oh, oh, oh," she took your own breath away.

You reach into the box of Heritage Os edged in green, and read its slogan: "The 'O' Stands For Organic." Your teeth crunch a handful of brown toasted rounds of "ancient grains," and maybe in eating "kamut, quinoa, & spelt," you're tasting a life before vowels.

9:03 by your watch. You should call her. A dental technician. "I've got feelings," she had said, implying you had none. You had repeated her word, "feelings," feeling your throat vibrate, hearing the "s" hissing, pushing back that serpent sound at her until your breath had quit.

What's to prevent the final "s" on "Heritage Os" from peeling off the cardboard box and floating through the dry air and sticking to the back of your hand?

Because it's a consonant, and you have *vowelitis*! There are no comparables. Maybe you can give your name to a new disease, and become immortal. And dead. The doctors always get the credit, and no one blames them when they say over your mother's morphined body, "We can't do anything more."

You bend over, and roll up your pantleg. Did you blink, or was that a vowel movement? No, but there's nothing wrong with a few laughs. You cover it up again. Will Dr. White approach the vowel area with his hand, and ask you to cough?

How can you be so sure it *is* a vowel when you can't really see it, and are afraid to touch it? She said, "You know everything," when you fixed her toaster plug. She said, "You know everything," when she opened her purse for the hexagonal key.

You have revenue figures, the square footage, two photographs, but no comparables for a nonconforming duplex in an area zoned for single family dwellings. You've heard of people catching colds, starting to snore, finding lumps of cancer . . .

It could be a consonant you got in that fleshy area near the right knee. Would it be productive for you to recite the whole alphabet? No.

The Mortgage Department of the Royal Bank wants you to complete that assessment today. You put on your heavy coat. In your first outdoor breath you swallow down a shard of freezing wind. And think you notice a patch of warmth near where your leg hinges. But you could be wrong.

On the street you try to watch exactly how you take bits of the winter air into your body. And you hold onto the invisible outside for a long while. When you breathe back out, you keep staring at your own heat.

Then you see a yellow tanker truck go by with the word "inflammable" painted on its rounded sides, and think it must mean the same thing as "flammable" and wonder about the extra letters it conveys.

Inside your '91 Toyota you wait for the engine to warm. Your right hand presses the button of the glove compartment, and scrabbles around inside for a tape that hasn't been played for years. You insert The Byrds into the mouth of the tape player, and twist the volume knob so far down the music is pretty much inaudible. Because mostly, you're remembering those separate voices singing their vowels and consonants into the same place.

You should go fill in some numbers. After the bearded Dr. White and his stainless-steel instruments check out what you're carrying. Your car phone is so cold your fingertips stick to the moulded plastic for a second. But what will you say if you call and she answers? Tell her about the letter that's maybe eating into your leg? She shares the alphabet with you, and could be suffering from the same disease of the flesh. Sitting with two hands just above the steering wheel, you remember how her yelps of love were so loud in your ears they scared you—and not much different from T.V. sound bites of torture.

And you wait and watch your mouth cloud the windshield.

Rain in the Laurentians

"Just call it a rain party, Gail."

"I'm so depressed."

"I'm the one who should be depressed, Mom. It's my birthday."

"I know that, Mark. What makes you think I don't know that? But how can we cram fifty-four people into this tiny cottage? Peter, who's that on the phone?"

"It's the Millers again. Somewhere near St. Saveur. They're still lost."

"Don't tell them how to get here. Where's Claire? She always disappears when she's needed. 'Hard work never killed anyone,' but our daughter's taking no chances."

Down by the lake Claire was trying to burn the end of a rope. The wind, heavy with rain, pushed past the curl of her hand, time and again snuffing out the paper matches. Tips now grey, they lay on the wooden plank, like Roman numerals.

Up beyond the cottage, past the birches and alders, the evergreens, the maples already edged in yellow and red, car doors closed, half-muffled, once, twice.

"Oh God, whose idea was this? It's raining even harder."

"Everyone will have a good time, Mom."

"The Laurentians in September are schizoid. It should either be sunny and summer and swimming, or snowy and winter and skiing. Sylvia! Come in. I'm so depressed."

"Oh, shut up, Gail. Hi, Peter. Happy Birthday, Mark! Here's your present. I passed the Millers. Heading back to town. Did you have a fight with them?"

"Are you crazy? They're just lost, thank God. I hear more people coming. Each car door slamming is like a bullet through my heart."

Claire pinched the corner of the match flap and dipped the flaring cardboard under the rope's frayed end. The flowered white strands puffed into burning light and shrank down to a sticky black mess.

"It's Mark's gang. Couldn't they have gotten into a minor car accident?"

"Gail!"

"Welcome. Come in out of the rain, all of you. Mark's delighted to see you. Hi, Jason. You made it. Claire must be down by the lake."

Claire threaded the carbonized tip of the rope through the plastic hole. Then, flexing her arm, she

86

wrenched the down-haul tight, and fixed the sail to the swivel.

"Now, Sylvia, don't faint when you see my mother. This'll be her first public appearance since her face lift."

"How old is she anyway?"

"Seventy-three. She lost two pounds of wattle. She used to walk past mirrors and say, 'That isn't me.'"

"It must be painful."

"My father used to call her 'glorious Gloria.' She even had a lip-lift."

Claire, holding the wishbone boom of the sail against her left hip, waded into the cold lake. The rain was blowing out.

"Mark, could you see who's at the door? I have to ice your birthday cake. How are your father's cataracts, Sylvia? Peter, can you shuck some of the corn? All the teenagers are goofing off, as usual. They must think this is a party."

"I think it's cute, Gail, the way they're playing charades. You know, I'm worried about Dad driving now. He really can't see anything."

"First. One word."

"Yesterday we were stopped, waiting for the light to change, and he pointed across the intersection and said, 'Look at that new hospital.'"

"A movie."

"I stared and stared, but there was nothing there, Gail."

"Butt. Head. Smash!"

"I swear, I thought he had gone crazy."

"Beating your brains out!"

"When I drove through the intersection, he said, 'Oh, it's a parked bus!'"

"RAM-bo!"

"Are we going to end up like that, Gail?"

Claire locked the sail to the board with the universal.

"It's wall-to-wall people in here."

"O.K. Everyone applaud. The Millers have finally made it! Where did you get that blonde wig, Sandra? It's hysterical. Let me try it on Bob! Why are your wearing sunglasses?"

"The only way to deal with reality is to deny it exists."

"Is there a problem, Mark?"

"The toilet wouldn't flush."

"Quick, give me a Valium, quick. What do you mean? We spent a fortune this summer on plumbing and drainage fields, Sylvia, only to be told last week by a government inspector, after everything was all filled back in, that the work was no good, and, of course, our friendly contractor had disappeared, and then this monstrous hulk of a guy—who did the actual digging— shows up, says he wasn't paid, and threatens to cover our place with boulders and chicken-shit. I'm so depressed."

"Everything's working fine. I just re-attached the chain to the handle."

"Isn't my son wonderful?"

"Why do all the boys want to try on my wig?"

"You look cute, Jason. What are you doing later tonight?"

Outside, Claire slid a freckled knee onto the hard, abrasive surface of the board.

"And here's Mom . . ."

For a moment Claire stood sideways on the rock-

88

ing board, slick with rain, then reached down towards the floating knot.

"No one expects very much from politicians, but the government is both corrupt and incompetent. It should only be one or the other. Isn't that right, Gloria?"

"She's fallen asleep. The drive must have exhausted her."

"Where's Claire?"

"Do you think it will clear up?"

"Open your presents, Mark."

Pulling the bright sail out of the lake, and then grasping the rough tubular boom near the mast, she headed for the far shore.

Jason and Mark stepped through the sliding door, out into the rain, where a tub of beer sat on the deck. They watched the lone windsurfer cutting across the dimpled lake, under the dark grey sky.

"Sylvia, did you see above her lip, where the freckles were scraped off? It doesn't look like skin anymore."

"They take away the outer layer, and what's left . . . "

"Let me see that birthday card, Mark."

"You're supposed to wear it. Look, it's got a hole for the nose. It's an old man's face. Put it on. Mark, you look twenty years older, like Peter. Actually, Sylvia, everyone says how young Peter looks. No one *ever* says how young I look. Pretty soon they'll think we're mother and son."

"It's not fair how men don't age like us. They cop out and die."

"Maybe I can luck into a plane crash. Isn't this rain ever going to stop?"

"Every time I turn around, someone else is disappearing into the bathroom with that wig on, to look at themselves in the mirror."

Coming about, Claire looked back into the blowing rain, across the lake to the far cottage, and jammed two cold toes against the mast-lock.

"It's like she's wearing a mask. The wallows and bulges around the hair-line."

"What's that?"

"It's the burglar alarm on Bob's Audi—he can't figure out how to turn it off."

"Is it ever going to stop?"

"He must be getting drenched out there."

"I'm wondering about Claire."

"Did you hear about the three ladies who got together for tea? The first one comes in, sits down, says 'Aiee!' The second one comes in, sits down, says 'Aiee!' The third one says, 'I thought we weren't going to talk about our children.'"

She rounded the point, and the cottage disappeared.

"Bob, you managed to turn it off."

"'The rest is silence.' I would have drowned out in that rain if it weren't for my baseball cap. You keep saying you're depressed, Gail, but do you realize it is now thirty years since I hit a home run? Nothing has ever felt as good as that moment in Little League, Peter. Not even sex. To hit the ball so hard, so squarely, so unmistakably, it's gone, beyond everyone's reach. The coach shouting, teammates yelling, everyone watching me circle the bases. Nothing has equalled that thrill."

"Bob, have another beer."

"Sometimes when I lecture I astonish myself with a brilliant phrase or insight, and I wish my students

90

would leap up, clapping and cheering madly, while I circle the desks."

Slanting past the weeds and the rocks, Claire planed above the roiled dark water. The board hummed with vibrations that travelled up her wet legs.

"Only a fool would use waxed dental floss."

"What do you mean? The unwaxed stuff gets caught in your fillings. Any moron knows that!"

"If you used the unwaxed string, stupid, you wouldn't need fillings."

The sailboard shot across the water-ski lane, ripping free a yellow buoy.

"I thought Mark fixed it."

Claire couldn't unclench her hands. She had been holding the wishbone boom too tightly.

"I heard she lost her virginity."

"Did she look under the bed? Behind the fridge?"

All at once Claire was cold, squinting into the rush of rain.

"Who are you?"

He had the body of a wrestler. A rope held up his pants. Hair bristled from his nose.

"What do you want?"

Her fingers had gone numb. It was a long way back.

"You're not welcome here."

She would have to return. Claire had reached the northern end of the lake. The little river, now big with rain, had cut new lines into the sandy beach.

His vinyl running shoes had left hundreds of tiny mud triangles on the floor.

"What do you want?"

He stood next to the dining-room table, eyeing the hot corn stacked high, the two glass rectangles of steaming lasagna, the wide bowl of green salad, the bottles set up like bowling pins.

"You've really filled out, Mark. Have you been doing weight-training?"

"Bob, take off your wet sunglasses. Mark's over there by the deck. That man you're talking to is someone else, a stranger."

The wind had shifted. It would be a long run home.

"A home run, Peter. I remember the fat end of the bat sending the ball right over the pitcher's head, over the centre-fielder's glove, over the red flags. Over. I'm not asking for fireworks exploding from the scoreboard."

"I'm not paying twice."

Running before the wind, Claire could see the rocky point in the smeary window of the sail.

The huge man stood next to the birthday cake, rocking slightly, mute.

She fought for a tricky balance, ignoring sore shoulders, tired arms, dead fingers.

"The contractor was supposed to pay you out of the money we paid him."

There was the point. Claire fell.

"Sir, will you . . ."

"Ma, stay out of this."

Claire heaved the heavy sail out of the lake.

"Sir, will you accept a cheque for half of what your contractor owes you?"

The house was again visible. The familiar diving raft was coming up quickly, with the dock just beyond.

The man pinched his nostrils shut, and nodded.

She glided in, and flung the sail down.

Jason waved to Claire from the sun-deck.

The rain had stopped.

Gloria's hand, wrinkled and spotted with brown, shook a little as it wrote out the cheque, but steadied as she handed it to the form looming above her.

Claire let Jason wrap her shivering body in a blanket. He followed her inside, where she paused next to the fireplace.

The stranger, holding the cheque in both hands, brushed past her.

"Come on, Mark. Open your presents."

"Where have you been?"

There was a low growl outside, of a truck starting.

Her hand was cold and tingling. With a long match, she lit the fifteen candles on her brother's cake.

Exhibit B—Black notebook

EXPERIENCE THE MYSTERY

With the flat midmorning light and the overlapping head-
lands, it's difficult for me to match the various forested
slopes to the sun-washed lines of the map fluttering on
my lap. Far off alone to the left must be — with cheap
symbolism — Lost Island, which — with some obvious
irony — is easily locatable. I am headed south in a light
following wind on board a converted tugboat, the *Auklet*,
along with a restless partner, another couple, the skipper,
and one crew member. Anthony Island, a UNESCO World
Heritage Site, which was formerly (and is again) known
to the natives as Sgaan Gwaii, is three days away, and the
intended subject of my travel article.

"As flat as piss on a platter."

"Is that an old nautical expression?"

I notice the way that Chris is already coming on to Pat, with the comments, the looks, the bottle of beer grasped around the neck, gesturing at the sea. To the east, in the direction of the mainland, immense dark-blue waters slide towards us. A huge flutter of blankness, with any landfall too distant for the eyes.

There are no small craft warnings on north coast waters. The area is always considered to have a small craft warning.

Though cruising here for the first time, I half-remember this watery place where missingness aches, pinching at the flesh. Seated adjacent to someone else's body, I wonder how absence can be so palpable, and draw a square bracket in the notebook: [ ].

ABSORB THE ATMOSPHERE
OF AN ANCIENT HAIDA VILLAGE

Glad to have worn high gumboots, I step out of the skiff into the clear, shallow water, holding the white pamphlet and the camera. Walking up the pebbly beach at Skedans Point, I feel the strangeness of *land* — its un-rocking falseness. So quickly do humans acclimatize, forgetting what the body knows best. I watch Dale help Pat and Alex out of the bow of the boat. The native Watchman, seated in the webbed aluminium chair, next to some driftwood logs and six empty cans of gas, rises slowly to greet us, and then leads our group along the village path, past the leaning poles that had once been painted red and black, but are now just grey wood with yellow-brown moss. Where long ago the cedar houses had stood, low spruce trees partly fill deep rectangular depressions in the earth. Bending sideways, I can make out (maybe) the eyebrows of a bear carved into a fallen cedar log, whose gently rotting wood sprouts seedlings and shoots of grass.

The black bears here are among the largest in North America. Their snouts tend to be longer, the jaws and teeth heavier. Some believe this is because they spend more time chewing hard-shelled creatures in the intertidal zone.

I note, involuntarily, that Chris is eating more than a fair share of the food at this hospitable gathering in a modern Bighouse.

"The radio says you won't have following north-westerlies much longer."

"We were hoping to ride them all the way down to Sgaan Gwaii."

On this combined working and pleasure trip, I had resolved not to get cross at tiny details, but, even on arrival at the Sandspit Airport, I became foolishly irritated because Chris's look of indifference had dissuaded me from buying a beautiful argillite pendant.

"It's hard to imagine raiding parties paddling their dugout canoes from way up here, near Alaska, across hundreds of miles of stormy open water, all the way south to Vancouver Island."

"About a hundred years ago some of our people went all the way down to Victoria to meet the white leaders."

Always feeling trapped in these discussions of red (right) and white (wrong), I stand up. "Thank you." Eager to get outside again, I cross the room to the small table where a large woman presses down a metal stamper on the last page of my "Watchmen Basecamp Passport."

"Slaves were treated as part of the family."

Have I heard correctly? Humans have an endless gift for justifying. Walking back along the path towards the shore, I hold the white pamphlet by its spine, thinking it's strange to be admitted formally to a place that on the map of Canada is undifferentiated by colour. I had always assumed this island to be a part of my own country. Touching the embossed, ink-less name with its circling letters, "Kuna," I wonder if a blind person could read the name for this site. An empty village now, but older than the nation with its white flag and fallen red leaf. Nearby, a fat raven calls out, with its nearly human voice.

That pendant which attracted me so much at Sandspit had both a raven and an eagle, the two birds which divide Haida kinship into clans. Its strong designs telling you who not to marry.

On this narrow point of land, almost hidden among the fast-growing spruce, is a cedar pole with long, parallel grooves cut vertically into the wood's circumference. I am struck by how much these decorative lines resemble those of columns. Tilting the camera, focusing on the mortuary pole, I try to frame the cedar's full height, and — click — imagine the long-ago canoe trip to Victoria and back, thinking of how the exhausted native paddlers must have carried with them on that endless journey homeward the shape of the new government building, and its white Grecian pillars.

REMOTE BEACHES

Leaving the *Auklet* behind in the skiff's wake, Chris, Dale, and I motor in the late light towards Vertical Point, its bay almost waterless.

The difference between high and low tide on the islands can be up to 24 ft. (7.5 m.)

Nearing the wet rocks, Dale slows the small boat. There, just an arm's length away, is a bright orange jellyfish, two feet across. Very leisurely, it swims out to sea.

"That's a Lion's Mane jellyfish. It's toxic to touch. Even when dead."

I peer into the shallow water for a minute, before getting out with the new tent, a sleeping bag, and the two-way radio. Wading quickly onto the drying rocks. Just beyond the slippery stones of the bay, a doe and a fawn are browsing in a meadow.

"We have the highest quota for hunting deer in the province."

"Why so many?"

"Bambi destroys the cedar. The Haidas need it to make their poles, houses, baskets, canoes, everything."

Dale drifts out, waves good-bye, then roars back towards the ship, the prop slicing up the placid black water. Chris and I drop our gear on the grass where the deer have been feeding, and swat at a dark fog of mosquitoes. I yank the tent out of its snug bag and look for the corners as Chris snaps the bungee-linked aluminium tubes into three long, springy curves. There's blood on Chris's forehead where a mosquito has been squashed. Clicking the clips onto the hooped rods to suspend the tent, I notice a raven has landed on top of the garbage bag that contains our sleeping bags. With a sideways glance, the raven checks us out, then pecks through the black plastic in search of decaying food. Chris spits out what seems like a mouthful of flying insects, and hammers in a peg fiercely. At the dusky edge of the clearing, the two deer browse at some young spruce trees, rounding down their vertical shapes — bonzaiing them — though one skying branch has gotten away. Most of the evergreens have a deformed shape: a narrow base with a bulge six feet up, beyond the mouths of deer.

"Let's get this stuff inside before we're eaten alive."

"I hope we're not going to get chewed on all the way down to Sgaan Gwaii."

I jerk the flap up, watch the black bird fly off, over the grey sea. Stooping inside, I drag the sleeping bag in, place it parallel to the other one. Chris zips shut the netting, and tugs off the blue gumboots, while I test the radio, adjusting the squelch button to keep the staticky noise out, then turn off the power. Chris, swinging the flashlight at mosquitoes, lunges into the sleeping bag, and turns away.

ARE YOU INTERESTED IN SEA LIFE?

My brain knows all those mountainous green islands to starboard can't be moving. But my eyes insist. And my body is getting sick from trying to believe both at the same time. But even half a Gravol pill would put me to sleep.

Winds opposite a strong tidal current cause waves to steepen. . .

"Make a fist and bend your hand. See these two long flexor tendons coming down from your wrist? Here and here."

Pitching wildly up and down, I try not to watch Chris cradling Pat's arm, playing doctor. It's so disloyal of Chris when my own stomach feels queasy.

"Measure down three middle-finger widths from the wrist crease, and press between the two tendons with the thumb, like this. That's the acupressure point called *nei-kuan*. Try it now, on the other hand."

"Like this?"

"Do you feel any better?"

"I feel like a contortionist."

Chris grasps both of Pat's wrists.

"They've now invented a wrist-stabilizer for sailors that's like a pair of watch-straps that push down for you, so both your hands can be free."

I have to wonder if it's jealousy or the choppy sea that's churning my stomach.

Dale strides back to the stern and gets out a hand-held line, a silvery weight and a pink hoochie on its end.

"We're nearing a shoal that's a good fishing spot for halibut. I'll drift the *Auklet* over it. Anyone interested?"

Jigging from a rocking boat is about the last thing I want to do, but it might make good copy, and could be a distraction. I stagger up from the deck chair.

"Let out the line, and when the weight hits bottom, jerk up like a wounded fish. Wear this glove, and if it's a halibut, don't catch a finger in the line."

I unspool the thick clear filament from the wooden bobbin, watch the weight flash down into the depths. It's like flying a kite in the wrong direction. I feel a slight shudder, jerk hard, and start hauling the line back in. Flipping the square wooden bobbin over and over, over and over. Speeding towards the *Auklet* is a small brown rockfish. Half-embarrassed, I swing it out into the air, and up over the railing. A fat, spikey face lies on the deck, breathing hard. Its macaroni-like intestines made visible by the jig hook that caught in the belly. I think of retching, but am strangely calm as Dale kneels to cut the hook free. The little brown bomber, brought up from depths too fast, has a shiny round thing in its mouth. Between its lips, a solid white bubble.

"That's the flotation device. Like an air-bag."

Dale casually throws the dead fish overboard. With a mixture of nausea and excitement, I again heave the weight and dancing hoochie over the side, noticing that Chris is now looking pretty interested in what might come out of the ocean next, and has let go of Pat's *nei-kuan* pressure point. There's a solid shudder on the line that's resting in my gloved hand. I jerk, begin pulling in steadily, turning the bobbin over and over, with Chris breathing licorice over my shoulder, and Dale coming back from the wheel to see. For an instant, the large orange blotch in the sea looks like a Lion's Mane jellyfish, but, submarining closer, it becomes a vividly orange snapper. I lift the big fish with its distended belly up into the air, and drop it down hard on the deck to excited shouts. As we all look, the stunning orange-red colour of the snapper fades. Turns to a very pale ochre.

"It must be shock."

"It must be six pounds."

Dale takes out a pointed knife and stabs it twice behind the eye. Once deep inside its quivering mouth.

"I've seen a halibut move two hours after its heart's been cut out."

101

Uneasily, I take the gutting knife from Dale
"People in holds have been killed by two-hundred-and-fifty-pound dead halibut flopping over on them." Wanting to avoid the snapper's scaly points, hesitant to stick a thumb in its soft gleaming eye for a better grip, trying to time the rocking of the waves, scared that the body which is turning orange again will move, I make the first cut. A quick slice behind the head with the bendy knife. Now running it softly along the notches of the backbone, all the way to the tail fin. Out of curiosity, before the filleting, I slice open the snapper's bloated belly. Grab out a small, half-digested rockfish. Bleached-white.

A UNIQUE BIOLOGICAL EXPERIENCE

The six of us from the *Auklet*, along with five kayakers from New Jersey, sit crowded together with flushed faces beside the hot-spring pool. Our hairy and hairless legs in the steaming water. Not far from the Arctic, our near-naked bodies lounge in more than tropic heat. I feel languid and anxious. The basic mental link between north and cold has disappeared in the steam. All around the wooden walkways and the dirt paths to the outdoor hot pools, the vegetation has an equatorial lushness. In defiance of the map, Hotspring Island is a torrid microclimate. And this water, much too hot. I try to cool down by thinking of hypothermia.

. . . *the loss of body heat, or lowering of the deep body core temperature, is serious. Put the casualty in a sleeping bag or blankets with one or two persons, with upper clothing removed.*

All at once Dale glides under and comes up smiling. Wet, curly red hair next to my hot toes.

CUSTOM ADVENTURE TOURS

Using the late light of summer up north, we have pulled up anchor, and are headed through Burnaby Narrows on the rising tide. I am sitting up front with Dale and Bernie.

"There're some Rhinoceros auklets. Do you want the glasses?"

"Thanks." Small black and white birds with short bills and tails, and a rapid wingbeat.

"See that white 'horn' of feathers? There, at the base of the beak."

Through the binoculars the horn looks solid. I can understand where the name came from. Bernie steps outside and reappears on the bow. Crouches down and stares, as Dale guides the *Auklet* through this long narrow stretch of water. At times the branches of the evergreens feel close enough to touch. Ahead, in the shallow water, a rock outcropping from the shore comes two-thirds of the way across. Impassable. Any further forward movement would be reckless. Bernie jabs an index finger to starboard. Impossible to navigate here, I reckon.

"I have to line up those two white pickets on the banks to find the channel groove."

Tense, I expect each moment to hear the crunch of rock against the wooden hull. On wings with serrated edges, an eagle glides past. In the dimming light a deer on a low hill watches, while the *Auklet* zig-zags through the rocks. On the grassy shore to the left (port) is a hippie

103

shack, abandoned. Dale's hand on the polished spokes spins the wheel rapidly, turns the ship sharply. . .

By the time we anchor south of Burnaby Narrows, and barbecue dinner, it's dark except for the moon, and too late to pitch the tent on shore. And I have somehow ended up alone again with Dale, this time at the stern of the *Auklet*. Chris must be up forward, in the head.

"Do you want to help me set the crab trap?"

I nod, and climb into the waiting skiff, taking the blue plastic wire cage that Dale hands down, then the striped float attached to a line, and finally the pungent bucket with the heavy head. Some of the blackened skin of the tasty red snapper we cooked for dinner is still left on the grill. In this smaller boat the two of us motor back towards the Narrows.

Then, under the moonlight, Dale cuts the engine, and we drift on the tide. I look on as Dale's strong hands fail to pry open the snapper's mouth. Rigor mortis has set in already. Is this the ambiance for a shipboard romance?

The mouth has now been pried open. Dale inserts a piece of rope and ties a knot, then, from the top of the blue cage, suspends the bodiless head. The four doors can only open in. I attach the float. Together, we lower the trap into the ocean. Could a crab that's outside rescue its trapped companions simply by holding a door open with a claw? A dumb question. A raven would be smart enough to figure it out. I ask Dale: "If you were a Haida, would you be an eagle or a raven?"

"Remember that pendant at Sandspit you liked a lot? Probably a bit of both. You?"

"Maybe I don't want to know. I don't like to think of myself as either a predator or a trickster."

Dale laughs, rinses both hands in the salt water.

Was it at Windy Bay that I had seen two ravens carved together on a board, signifying a marriage against clan traditions? The outboard engine sputters and catches, and Dale steers towards the *Auklet*.

Chris, waiting by the stern rail, snags the coil of rope that Dale tosses up.

"Are we going to have crab meat for breakfast?"

"That or Kellogg's Corn Flakes."

"The others are already in their bunks."

Chilled, I glance at the two sleeping bags unrolled on the deck.

"Good night."

"I hope it doesn't rain."

"See you in the morning."

Taking the green toothbrush from Chris, I squeeze a striped dab of toothpaste onto the bristles. Chris scrubs much faster than me, but at the same instant we spit over the side. Bubbled mouthfuls shine on the dark water. Chris turns away.

As I tug off the yellow gumboots, Chris slides into the closest sleeping bag, all clothes on. I jump into the other one, and kick both legs up and down vigorously. Tired, but not much warmer, I hear a loud, rhythmic banging. Feel a hot embarrassment for Pat and Alex. And envy at their urgent, public desires.

BINOCULARS AND CAMERAS ARE RECOMMENDED

I wake to hear Pat and Alex going at it again! Pulling the sleeping bag up over the head doesn't muffle their hungry, insatiable rhythm. How much longer, I wonder, can they keep up this shuddering, brutal sex? Like a head being rammed against the cabin's wooden wall.

The door between the stern deck and the cabin opens. Dale stares down at us.

"Sorry for waking you. I have to re-tie the skiff."

The knot Chris tied last night in the dark must have loosened. I have to laugh. The bow of the small boat has been swinging out, and then banging back hard against the rubber tire attached to the side of the *Auklet*. Chris struggles up, that familiar clump of blonde hair covering the left eye. Dale ties a clove hitch around the metal railing, then two half-hitches jerked tight.

"If you two are interested, now's the best time to check out the sea life in Burnaby Narrows. It's low tide."

"Let's go then."

I want to stay inside the cozy sleeping bag. But, thinking there might be more material for the article, reach out a hand, feel the inside of a clammy boot. Already Chris has picked up the Minolta. Dale undoes the knot, and helps Chris, then me, into the skiff.

In the early light we idle towards the Narrows. I can make out the striped buoy that marks the crab trap.

"We'll get it on the way back."

The sea bottom very visible in this very shallow water. All around the small boat is intertidal life. A shag carpet of shells.

"Wow!"

"Look there."

A stunning superabundance. Dale shuts off the motor, and then brushes past me to lift the curved blades of the prop clear of the drying ocean floor. Drifting now, back towards the *Auklet*, over the thick beds of

clams, the starfish everywhere, long razor clams, giant
tufts and swatches of mussels, and some huge jellied
creatures with moonshell carapaces, abalone and turban shells, and a snakey swimming thing like a woman's old-fashioned black boa.

"A sea eel."

I watch Chris trying to photograph it all, shot after
shot. We're floating over too much unimaginable life.

Dale releases a pin, and lowers the prop back into
the deeper water we've drifted to.

"Let's go see what's for breakfast."

We speed over to the striped buoy. Dale hauls it
onboard, with its slimy rope where small, webbed starfish — blue, violet, purple — cling. The dripping cage
is thrown at my feet.

"What a haul!"

"They're too tangled up to count."

"These kind have to be at least four and a half inches
wide."

"That one must be eight inches."

A huge claw with barnacles grips at the blue plastic
that sheaths the wire cage. In the middle of the scraping, shifting mass, I see two crabs which are still feeding on the snapper's eyeless head.

The clunk of a gear change, and we're going full
throttle towards the *Auklet*.

"I count thirteen."

"And all large enough to keep."

As we swing alongside the ship, Dale shouts up at
Bernie: "Fill that pail with sea-water, and then put the
big pot on to boil."

Dale opens the lid of the trap. One crab crawls out
towards my gumboots. Chris continues clicking away,

while Dale picks it up by the hindmost legs and tosses the strange creature up on deck to Bernie, who catches it with bare hands, then plops it into the waiting bucket.

Just then, Pat and Alex emerge from the cabin — sleepily stare at crabs splashing into the pail. So full now, the crabs are landing on top of each other.

"We should get underway. Who wants to cook?"

Feeling absurdly possessive of the thirteen crabs, I say, "I will."

"And I'll make a Louis sauce."

I grab the damp railing, and climb aboard the *Auklet*. One large claw extends out over the pail's rim, opening and shutting against the air. I pick up the handle, feel the plastic sides of the bucket straighten up, and come forward to the galley lugging the weight of crabs and sea-water, one eye on the menacing pincer. A big pot bungeed to the wall is already heating. I remember the pool at Hotspring Island, and the proximity of pleasure to pain. The steam rising. For the crabs this is going to be pretty unambiguous.

"Cook only half of them at a time."

"We should get to Rose Harbour tonight."

Avoiding the claw, I pick up the half-escaped crab by a rear leg. Not wanting to throw a live thing into the boiling water. But my hot fingers let go. I tremble at the slight hiss, see the crab turning pink.

Now another. Another, and another, to get it over with fast. I am becoming a hard-shelled creature, just counting. This seventh, and last one, of the first batch.

"Look!"

Even as it's turning red, the big crab with barnacles on its enormous claws is trying — like we would! — to climb out.

"Look! Over there."

"See that hooked dorsal fin? It's a minke whale."

I have picked up a wooden spoon, am trying to keep the crab under the white bubbling water — very badly wanting to make its death what it isn't: instantaneous.

"It must be twenty-five feet long."

"Black, with a pointed head. And there's a diagonal patch of white on its flipper."

"A minke whale?"

It must be dead now.

"Yeah. It's got lots of other names, in places like Japan and Russia, Norway. Peru. It's hunted everywhere now that the really big whales are on the endangered species list. Here, do you want to take a look?"

I lay the wooden spoon on the stovetop, and take the binoculars. Scanning the wide, cool water. "I can't see anything." Still hearing hot burbling.

"It hasn't surfaced again."

"They can hold their breath for up to twenty minutes."

Dale flips the guidebook open and reads: "little piked whale, sharp-headed finner, *koiwashi kujira*, *rorqual pequeno, maly polosatik, minkehval, balaenoptera acutorostrata*."

"O.K., O.K. Too many names is like having no name at all."

I smell delicate flesh cooking, look down at the boiling pot, and imagine the minke whale diving with all its names into cold water, so deep and far its gleaming black sides reach the coast of Peru. Breathless. The dead animals crowd each other in the iron pot.

The next step should be easier because I have done

it before. Just ladle them out of the boiling broth, tear off the legs and claws, break open the sharp, tough shells, rip off any tentacles, snatch out all gut parts that don't show white, and then crack the bodies in two.

"Pigeon guillemots."

"They're funny birds with those bright feet."

I turn to the square window, and see one of the dark-grey sea-birds with white flecks on its wings coming in like a strange torpedo. Its webbed feet an amazing orange-red. It lands on a wave, a needle fish in its mouth.

"Better swimmers than flyers. Their wings are adapted to push water. They can dive down a hundred metres."

"They look ready to eat."

"The sauce is ready."

I balance a crab on the wooden spoon, lift it out into a broad bowl.

"Where are we now?"

"Skincuttle Inlet."

"I'm starving."

I move one cooked crab after another onto the growing pile of corpses in the stainless steel bowl.

"They look delicious."

I rinse off both hands, then breathe at my upraised fingertips, worried that the smell of crab meat will stay under the nails forever.

Everyone else is seated at the table. "These are delicious."

I notice that Dale is using the crab's own leg as a tool to pick the flesh out of the joints. A curious creature that helps eat itself.

WILDERNESS

The beach seems little nearer now than when I plunged in. After the hot sunshine, and the boiling, I had imagined that the cold water would feel like a gift.

Survival in cold water: As a general rule you can swim less than 1/10 of the distance you could in warm water.

Dale and Pat and Alex are nearby in the skiff if I need help. But diving into the ocean was still a rash thing to do, when a Lion's Mane jellyfish could — right now — be swimming towards my gleaming black swimsuit, and bare limbs. It's hard to make progress when you're looking back constantly, or to the sides, or peering down into dark depths. But the beach stones may be getting closer. The rising tide, I realize, is now helping wash my tight, cold body towards the island. Head down, eyes open, I stroke more confidently, kicking hard at the dark-blue sea. Even feeling pleasure at this heavy fatiguing of muscles, working to push my head through the buoying water, all the way to Peru if I wanted. But needing now to come up for some air.

"You're almost there."

Immersed once again, I look down at the sea weed and clam beds. Won't have to hold onto this breath for twenty more minutes. Already, the others are dragging the boat up on the sunlit stones. And I can touch the bottom.

I stand, and wade ashore to where Dale is tying the small boat to a large rock.

"Your hair's like a raven's."

Dale's is thickly red, curly, and dry. The trickster self gone? Flirting openly now. Alex and Pat, halfway towards the bay's far point, search for shells.

From the open neck of the short-sleeved green shirt,

Dale pulls out a silver chain, shows me the pendant. Grasping it with two hands, lifting it, ruffling some red curls, Dale swings the argillite carving up into the sky, and then lowers it down over my wet head. The black stone warm against my chest.

I follow Dale up the beach to a large cedar tree.

Pat and Alex are only two hundred yards away, with binoculars. Hunting for brick-red turban shells, or perhaps moonshells whose clock-wise whorls make a nipple on a tiny breast, or maybe seeking abalone with glistening insides, a sea-eel. . .

I think briefly of Chris with a headache and a sunburn back on the *Auklet*. Then kneel down behind the wide cedar with Dale on a bed of moss. Already I am half-freed of my wet suit. Beginning to hear all the minke names: the little piked whale with its hooked dorsal fin, *koiwashi kujira,* the sharp-headed finner, *rorqual pequeno,* and *maly polosatik,* whaling away, the *minkehval,* diving rhythmically, and *balaenoptera acutorostrata,* nearly lost in the depths, while on my pale chest the eagle and the raven fly up and down.

A VIBRANT ECONOMY

I again throw the empty pail attached by a rope into the *Auklet*'s wake. Trying to get salt water as we travel, without being pulled in. But the plastic pail just rides on top of the water like a toy boat. Waiting to be swamped. I glance across at Dale.

"To get some you have to throw it in upside-down."

I try this illogical move, and it works immediately — a heavy tugging weight at my shoulder.

Chris, who holds a small mauvish bottle, doesn't

respond to my smile. About ten minutes ago Chris found this object washed up on the beach at Raspberry Cove. I haul the sloshing pail of water on board, and empty it on the grey-white bird-shit stuck to the deck. Some of it washes away through the scuppers. Chris is now rolling the worn cylindrical glass between thumb and forefinger. Washed by sea-water and brushed by sand. Chris's finger encircles the slender neck, feels at the thin, unbroken lip on top, touches at its opening.

"Maybe a Japanese fisherman kept opium in this mysterious little bottle."

Pat takes the bottle Chris offers, and blows into its pale mauve shape.

"It doesn't look like a perfume bottle."

I am suddenly conscious of the small bulge of a pendant hanging under my t-shirt.

"We'll anchor in a few minutes, and go ashore for dinner. There are some great vegetable gardens at Rose Harbour. Tomorrow morning, we'll visit Anthony Island."

"Look over there. Some puffins."

"Where's my camera?"

"Are those tufted puffins?"

"No. Horned."

Alex, Bernie, and I get into the skiff with Dale for the first ride into shore. Chris and Pat wave goodbye from the deck-chairs.

"On the map, it says Rose Harbour isn't part of the South Moresby National Park Reserve."

"No, it's a blip in history from the sixties. And before the commune, it was a whaling station for B.C. Packers."

I look back at the wake from the outboard engine,

that's lengthening in a perfectly straight line from the
Auklet, where no people are visible. Ahead, the slope of
Rose Harbour, with three or four hand-built houses that
are hard to make out among the evergreens. The skiff
slows as rounded rocks appear in the water below, close
to the aluminium hull. Then a grating sound, as the
boat stops.

Getting out, I nearly step on a wedge-shaped thing.
An orange and dark-brown object. What I pick up is
rusted, four-sided, and very heavy.

A harpoon head. I note that its point has been
blunted by the corrosion of water, and the grinding of
rocks. Maybe it has been inside the heart of a whale. In
back of the harpoon is a hollow circle, where a shaft
once connected the iron arrow to a line, and men in
boats, and money.

DISCOVER

The six of us stand in the drizzle on Anthony Island.
Its village, Ninstints, has followed the curve of the bay.
The house structures mostly rotted away. Tongue and
groove for the broad hand-hewn vertical boards. One giant, mossy transverse beam remains, an end fallen to the
ground. But the other, still high up in its big, airy notch.

"Even this will be gone in twenty-five years."

The Watchman here at Anthony Island, or Sgaan
Gwaii, used a quotable phrase, "a living graveyard."
Introduced as Captain Gold, apparently he was once
known as Wanagun, and before that as Dick Wilson —
almost as many names as the minke whale. He has
drawn a hideous mosquito that covers the inside of his
wooden door, an exquisite and graphic reminder to

visitors to close the door!

Haida culture is a living and evolving culture.

I follow the Minolta lens out from Chris's face to the fawn lying in a grassy house depression.

Chris motions for me to pose in front of a glistening silver-grey pole, which has the remnants of three carved watchmen at its very top. No one alive here now, in what once was a village of four hundred. A cobweb of fog stretches between the cedar poles and some isolated house posts. Would the kids who once walked around here with their dogs have been scared of the mortuary poles? The high bentwood boxes held their dead grandparents in fetal positions along with a few valued possessions. Maybe in the village edged by sea and wilderness the presence of ancestors in the wet grey sky would give comfort.

Likely, these photographs will be spotted by rain.

"It's time to walk back."

Coming and going. I touch the sharp wet tips of evergreen sprouts. The dead spirits remained for a year in the funeral house before the erection of the pole, and the potlatch feasting, with its conspicuous gift-giving.

A few trees have recently been cut down to let in light to dry the totem poles out a bit, but there's no restoration as such — and these totems aren't totems, I remember — not ancestor worship, but clan allegiances, with all the carved animals linked to one of those two birds: the raven or the eagle. Vandals have chopped off a wooden raven's wing. And taken away the face of some other creature. Presence and absence. Flowering plants grow out of the mortuary poles.

Chris and I are the last ones starting back on the path to where the *Auklet* is anchored.

"Smile."

I turn, smile at the familiar blonde hair, and at the round glass of the camera lens.

"Did you get that Haida pendant?"

I don't know what to say. The truth solid and heavy. A stone around my neck. "Yes."

"I saw you liked it a lot, and decided to surprise you. But, by that time, our luggage was coming down the shoot and the Indian lady was headed outside to her pick-up truck. So I whipped out a hundred bucks and asked the skipper to catch her. This morning when I remembered, and asked for my money back, Dale told me you'd already gotten my gift."

"Yes."

A present, and an absence. A deceit to get what belongs to someone else.

"The jerk's already given it to you?" Both of Chris's hands clench into fists.

"Yes."

Quickly pulling out the beautiful pendant, I look down at the two carved images. Leaning forward, I kiss Chris's rainy face. Seduced by my own partner's gift. I hug Chris very close. "Thank you." For only a hundred bucks, my sexual affections have been bought.

I look over Chris's shoulder at the grey sea and hope the southeaster will blow the *Auklet* back to Sandspit in a hurry. Along with its pair of tricksters.

ACTIVE OUTDOOR EXPERIENCES

Seated across from each other in the *Auklet*'s stern, Chris and I watch as Sgaan Gwaii, or Anthony Island, with its whale-like hump, disappears into the sea and fog.

As if where we have been were only a mirage — "a marriage" — I jot down compulsively.

Chris picks the filleting knife off the deck and carefully places it next to the Minolta camera on the webbed seat of a folding chair.

With unlaced gumboots, and a grin for me, Dale steps over the door-sill, and thumps across the deck to the railing. When Dale turns, the three of us are spaced like the points of an equilateral triangle.

Everyone in your group should be within talking distance of each other.

As simple as ABC——

Orpheus: Time and Again

Having come down the shaded drive, I didn't enter like the others. And now all these figures who fell out of my awareness long ago are swarming up to greet me like buzzing, solid ghosts—like eager T.V. re-runs.

In this cavernous place, among drifting bodies and obscure faces, Mr. Yogi Smith presses forward, then passes. I flash on how he stumbled once during his biology class, cracking us up by saying "testicles" instead of "tentacles." But where's Erin?

A bald guy hands me an icy bottle of Moosehead. "Orville. It's me, Ralph. Your boyhood buddy." Like some doom bass chord, the cliché about high school reunions is there right in my face. Is everyone's life trashed by forgetting? The nice thing about Alzheimer's is forgetting you've got the disease. Ralph, feeling at his round pink scalp with an air of disbelief, introduces me to his third wife.

And barging in is Jim Winters, the fat loud-mouth who organized this bad-vibe event. Winters begins interrogating me, pumping my hand with a Kiwanis Club enthusiasm, with the arm he used to peg out runners trying to steal second. "Is that really you, Orville? Where's your trumpet?"

"Guitar, man. I played the lead guitar track for Sinatra once." Why am I hyping myself, and why's my voice coming out falsetto?

"Now I remember. The electric *lyre*. Well, you're looking fine, Orville."

"You're looking wickedly prosperous, man, but then I understand only the rich, or the skinny, attend these things." Enough with the edgy, unfunny wisecracks: Don't tell the C.A. joke. "I hear you're partners in the accounting biz, with Erin's husband?"

"Yes, but excuse me. I have to make a speech."

I'm drinking fast, hoping for a buzz when Mr. Makarov, my ex-basketball coach, stomps in front of my semizonked eyes, his black T-shirt stretched tight over massive pecs. Even yet his huge biceps could shot-put me half-way across this neatly clipped burb lawn, but his face is weirdly drained of blood. And he blanks out on me—has no memory of my two big free throws in the final minute. All of them wear name-tags, but I haven't scored one yet, and have to speak my two-syllable name out loud: "Or-ville"—which always sounds so uncool inside my head. Coach Makarov points at my beard as an excuse, and I tell him, "The nice thing about Alzheimer's disease is you get to meet so many new people."

The teachers were always ancient, but don't really look older twenty-five years later. But we do. Somehow we've warped into their age *then*—like their shadows, like some low-tech rip-offs. In this bluesoid scene, I hear the breathy modulations of Sandra Richardson beside me. The class flunk-out is talking of the AIDS hospice she has helped set up. Who would have guessed? Her throaty syllables emerge upbeat despite the sunless dude next to her in dark shiny pants, his thinness an un-chic wasting away.

In the woods once with Sandra, behind the school field on a warm Friday afternoon, having skipped the double period of Industrial Arts or Home Economics (back when things were assigned by gender), she let my quick, ignorant hands discover a woman's flesh at last. No riddle to her loving, so why wasn't *she* the woman who time and time again danced through my dreams? Her still generous "D" cups—thanks for the mammary—next to that shade of a man.

Would Erin bother to show? Not my scene, but now too late to split. Winters, the head honcho, bellows out his welcoming speech: "Little did I know when I was elected head of the grad committee I would be accepting a lifetime appointment."

He starts to peg questions at us: "Who has come the farthest?"

Half-unsure why I hopped a jet plane in L.A. to get me to this gig, I raise my hand, get a scattering of applause and congrats—like some lame, quasi-celebrity, half-remembered.

"Who has the oldest children? Any grandchildren?"

You can see bodies stiffen like corpses at Winter's bullying intimacy, but people keep sticking up their hands.

"Who has been married the most times?"

Ralph's scalp's flushed hot-pink by everyone's tabloid interest.

"Who has never been married?"

A dyke, a dude in a pimp suit I can't remember with an albino patch on his face, and me, that's it— our arms slow to rise, and out of sync. At seventeen I had my big break to open for the Jefferson Airplane tour and she . . .

On cue, Erin's laughter washes into my ears. Don't look back. It's like Chet Baker's trumpet: pearly seashells, half-open, flung ashore in glass-green waves that are breaking . . .

She starts towards me, arms bare, her silk-draped body still pulsing with good times and laughter. Only those long white gloves worn at the grad dinner are missing, and no neo-punk hair shave back then. She steps right past me. My grad date doesn't fucking know who I am!

I try to drain the third Moosehead.

She catches at my sleeve.

"Orv?"

Beer splashes into my lungs as I try to talk.

"How long have you had a beard?"

"Forever and a day, Erin."

Next to her is a man in a charcoal suit who looks younger than me. She introduces me to her husband. I hear myself saying, "What do you get when you put two accountants together?"

"What, Orville?"

"Caca."

Even delivering the punch-line, I feel lousy. Erin laughs brightly, like I hoped, but why do I have to put down the geek? The conversation turns to houses and children—that square, hardcore happiness I never wanted. But I'm staring at Erin's clown-like eyes with some of the helpless caring that once freaked me out. That probably sent me away, holding the body of my Stratocaster with acid-twisted love. This time she's the one headed for the exit, with a quick fluttering wave of her long fingers, and her husband clinging to her like some one-hit wonder, looking like death's shadow. Her elegant shoulders turn, and she's gone back into the ghostly past.

Left standing in the gloom of this huge, empty room, I hear some faint music that grabs at me, drags me down narrow wooden stairs to where a compilation of sixties hits comes out in the eerie silence of a Sony CD machine, all the notes scrubbed clean. Here, there are no fuzzy, shrill sounds of 45s wobbling around a spindle on red plastic inserts. Now only a cheesy greying sock hop in a windowless basement. Instead of the beer ad on the beach look, with bouncing babes and boobs, there's just tired blood, and images of dead meat. It is worse than unhip: you've been had.

Ralph and some of the other dudes lounge against the beige wall, eye-balling two fat-assed chicks on Prozac jiving together. The guys in the dim light joke about car crashes and blue balls—still too uptight to ask a girl to dance. But in the semidarkness, our teenage lives start coming back: you don't yet have the disease if you can remember the name Oppenheimer's. It was such a stupid, numb terror having to ask a girl to dance, even though she would just take your hand, and let you press her body casually against yours for as long as the music lasted.

Ralph lunges forward now, and within seconds a dozen bodies are on the lino floor, grooving to the insistent back-beat. My classmates are tangling up limbs and torsos. On the sideline, my arms feel useless without a guitar to hold, and the muscles of my face are getting sore from smiling like an unhip Bozo, at everyone and nothing.

The fluorescent lights flash off and on, and everyone laughs nervously, as if the adults had almost caught us *doing it* in the dark. Of course, it's Erin, at the top of the stairs, lips pulled open wide, her fingers flicking the switch. And when she skips down, she's just seventeen. Her grad dress was a shimmering of turquoise sequins, and I'd given her a corsage bigger than my heart.

"Erin, do you believe in *déja vu*? Erin, do you believe in *déja vu*?"

"Yes," she smiles. "Yes."

Holding her pliant body so close again, I find myself loving everyone in the room stupidly. To be dancing with her, circling the floor to a fab Beatles tune, hanging with all these people who tried out new lives together with us, makes me forget to be a smartass. Her up-turned, diamondy eyes. I could have stayed, sold life insurance, whatever. For better or worse. And even now I can imagine dancing right up the stairs with her, out of this dark room filled with friendly breathing ghosts, into a kind of dawn, mortgage, whatever. Some groupies, once, nearly tore me apart, but nothing has ever set my insides adrift like Erin's lips on mine.

123

As soon as the music stops, she lets go of my hand. The stone in Erin's ring throbs in my head. And the man in the charcoal suit is asking, "Erin, would you like to dance?"

Twenty-five years later she isn't going to save the last dance for me.

I climb to the top of the stairs alone. When I look back, Erin is bobbing among the dim forms below—all keeping a separate time to the same music. There's a twinge between my legs as I see her husband's arms around her like dark tentacles.

Outside, in the flowing night, my mouth falls open, and I begin singing the blues. And my eyes float with wetness, remembering the shape of happiness.

Tennis at Popham Beach

Here, in the piney woods, right next to their vacation cottage, with its rambling porch, huge clapboard front, and high gables, the paint stripped back to wood grain by salt winds, was the local court. What good fortune, Nancy thought. Tennis was an ideal diversion after a day of lying on the sand, of testing the cold waters.

"How should we play?"

"Two against two?"

Half-smiles and delayed laughter linked the party of four. All were glad to be near the ocean, in Maine again. They had driven hundreds of miles to be freed from their stressed urban lives.

Marvin led the way on to the hard surface, announcing, "Brian, you get to play with my wife. David and I will form a dynamic duo of father and son."

David, in his purple Mohawk, stared at the sea through the wire fence. The August sun had burned off the morning fog. The rocky island a mile beyond the curving beach looked an easy swim away. The earlier dingy browns of the dunes had dried a silver-grey. Tall grasses glinted next to the soft petals and hard red apples of wild roses.

There was a metallic rasp as Brian twisted open a can of balls. The bearded historian inhaled the whiff of newness, then fumbled, failing to hold three balls at once in his hand.

The four players began to warm up. Within minutes there were no more balls. An errant volley by Nancy had found the opening in the fence at midcourt, and David had twice hit what he called "A home run." When he slouched into the bushes to look for the yellow balls, his mother warned, "Watch out for the poison ivy!"

"What does it look like?"

"How should I know? But back in the 50s the Coasters had a big R&B hit called 'Poison Ivy'."

"Mom, I'm not in here playing fucking Trivial Pursuit."

Meanwhile, Marvin and Brian mimed an elaborate point with an invisible ball. As much as their own imagined acrobatics, the two men enjoyed sharing a twenty-year-old film reference to Antonioni's *Blow-Up*.

When David returned with three damp balls, the mosquitoes attacked. The whine of Stuka dive-bombers from war documentaries was a less welcome cinematic allusion the two men shared. There was a frenzy of unorthodox racquet swinging. Marvin had taken off the white hat, which was supposed to protect his balding, pre-cancerous scalp from the sun, and was beating himself about the shoulders. David gaped at a mosquito so bloated with his blood that it was struggling to stay airborne. Nancy screamed that chunks of her flesh were being ripped out by a green-headed insect whose jaws were roughly the colour, shape, and size of a crocodile's. Brian pondered the message on David's T-shirt: HAVE A NICE DAY SOMEWHERE ELSE.

All at once Marvin sprinted for the house in his bright white Reeboks. David, with crude chording on his racquet strings, mouthed the lyrics to a song by Suicidal Tendencies. Brian and Nancy discussed the odds of getting AIDS from mosquitoes.

"Actually, Nancy, the virus is very weak, even fragile, like your volleying."

"I guess it would wilt and die in seconds in the open air, if you exposed it."

A skull and cross-bones against a black background decorated the spray can that Marvin held at the edge of the court.

"What about the ozone layer?"

"You ecological wimp."

"Kill Nature!"

"Waste those mother mosquitoes!"

Marvin's slow, sweeping movements across the court formed the thick aerosol fog into a hovering, elongated "S." Brian was reminded of the brilliant cinematography of *Death in Venice*: the camera's languid panning had had the same hypnotic effect.

On the baseline, in a fury of slathering, Nancy immersed herself in liquid insect repellent. "I've lost five pounds in five minutes. These vampires can drink someone else's blood dry!"

"Let's play!"

On the rally for serve, Nancy's racquet flew out of her wet hand and cleared the net. Her husband ducked, then declared, "Out." It had landed wide of the doubles court.

"It didn't go over three times," Brian argued.

At last the set began.

Nancy served the opening game, slashing the ball at her husband and son, making them look inept for two points. At thirty-love she blasted a serve that hit the centre line for an ace. Her teenaged son just brushed his hand back through his Mohawk, while the father said, "Do this," and started bouncing up and down on his toes, shaking convulsively, as if under electro-shock therapy. Ignoring the obvious reference to Jack Nicholson in *One Flew Over the Cuckoo's Nest*, Brian felt flooded by sensations of well-being: the match had to be his, if already—in the very first game—the father was coaching his son. Warming thoughts of victory left him unprepared for Marvin's swift return of service. However, the ball struck Brian's graphite frame, nicked across the net, and angled cross-court for game point. Brian hoped that the others would believe his mis-hit volley was skilfully intended.

Marvin served next. He hit the ball with a tricky twist that he had learned last winter at a tennis clinic in Florida for fifteen hundred dollars. It was worth every penny, he thought, as his wife, mistiming the spin, hit the return through the gap at midcourt into underbrush. Her "Oh, Marvin!" was eerily close to her orgasmic voice. Having fooled his wife's bearded partner with the same left-handed twist, Marvin served again to Nancy, his ears alert. Again, he made her lose control. She flailed in helpless abandon. Her intense, repeated, "Oh, Marvin!" made her cries in bed sound paltry, even simulated. In a rage he smashed the ball right at Brian who could only protect his private parts, grateful for the racquet's outsized head.

"One all."

At the start of the third game, Brian hammered in three straight serves for winners. Each one had felt absolutely right. Forgotten were the troubles in getting here—the failed alternator making the aged car surge and die, and then the clanking scrape of the muffler on the Maine Turnpike, the whole Saab story, he had said, in a fine pun that the others had ignored. Now three straight winners. He had never done this before in his life. That such a feat had not occurred earlier in his personal history in no way contradicted this moment of triumph, any more than the Dark Ages invalidated the glory of the Renaissance that followed. But it was curious that the past had offered so few hints about the future. Could he hit four winners in a row?

In the toss upward the ball jerked free of his clawing hand in stricken flight. Brian's racquet swiped it into the bottom of the net. He recalled the cheese he had eaten for lunch. The doctor had spoken to him about lactose intolerance, and his inability to digest the sugar contained in milk products, but hard cheese wasn't supposed to give him diarrhoea. His second serve bounced before it reached the net. Then he remembered his young third wife, sulking in the cottage. Afraid to double-fault again, Brian patted in his next serve to

David who hit a hard shot at Nancy who popped it up into the air for Marvin's vicious swinging volley. "Great shot!" shouted Brian. Having lead forty-love, now in danger of losing his service game, he feigned praise, calculating that Marvin, out of hubris, would attempt to play beyond his level of skill. Sure enough, on the key point, Marvin tried to hit a topspin lob from deep in the corner, dribbling the ball off his partner's black running shoes.

"Two-one! I mean, one-two."

David hit every serve at full volume. Double faults alternated with aces in a monotonous, punk rhythm. At thirty-thirty, his father turned around. "Just get the second serve in, David."

David strummed his gut strings, while singing tonelessly, "Whatever I do just isn't good enough for you, is it?"

"Leave him alone, Marvin," Nancy shrieked at her husband.

David resumed his jagged serving. He aimed to get his father in the back, but missed, scoring an ace instead. Two double faults later, David began to see his father, hairy legs outspread and bristling arms upraised, moving back and forth along the net, as a white-bellied spider. He finally hit it.

"Three-one!"

The afternoon was getting hotter. Nancy wiped her Vuarnet glasses on her tennis skirt, then tucked a ball under her panties. Brian wondered at this casual physical intimacy between fuzz and flesh. He strained to follow the trajectory of her second serve to see whether the moisture from her body, by distorting the ball's perfect spherical balance, encountered extra air resistance, and imparted a spitball effect. A savage yellow blur to the head, cushioned only slightly by a head-band, dizzied Brian. Nancy feared that sweat was wash-ing away the insect repellent—and her mousse make-up that evened out her skin tones. Marvin whanged a cross-court winner, and, exultant, shook his fist at his son. "We're only this one service break down." David tugged at his earring. Nancy then turned aggressive, treating each subsequent point with the combativeness appropriate to a power lunch.

"Four-One!"

During Marvin's first serve there was an insistent, querulous beep. He wanted the point replayed, even after Brian had pointed out that it was Marvin's own electronic watch that had made the noise. Tracey's ap-pearance courtside in her second-skin bikini left the argument unsettled. Marvin was tossing the ball up again when Brian's wife pulled her bra top to one side to scratch at a mosquito bite. He flubbed his serve into the net. As he hit his second serve he thought she was going to scoop it . . .

"Out! Love-forty," Brian shouted.

"It's fifteen-all. You're like Waldheim. You lie about the past."

Brian wished to question, or to modify this histori-cal analogy, in order to set the record straight, to main-tain their lead in the game, and to impress Tracey, but he was worried that an enraged Marvin would chal-lenge him to a singles match. Then Tracey would see him as either a coward or a loser.

"Let's call it fifteen-thirty."

Marvin's next two serves were faults. Pain shad-owed his forehead as he recalled how awkward his old serve had looked on the videotape machine, and now, under pressure, he had reverted to that herky-jerky floundering. Fifteen hundred bucks blown away, he thought bitterly. Nancy, resenting Tracey's sleek chic and her high-rise topknot, swung fiercely at Marvin's demoralized serve, and skimmed an ungettable return past her son, who, in any case, stood catatonic at the net, his shaven scalp now a hot pink.

"At least look like you're trying, David."

"How things look. That's all you care about."

Nancy intervened from across the net, "It's not the U.S. Open, Marvin!"

Brian was mute. If he could only hold his serve now, he and his partner would win the set. Do what Stan Smith says: throw the ball slightly higher in tense situations to prevent hitting the ball into the net. But Nancy, holding her racquet like a fashion accessory, lost several points, repeating, "It's just for fun. It's not the U.S. Open." Brian analyzed that she was trying to make peace between her husband and son by sabotaging *his* serve, in front of Tracey. The game was virtually over and lost when he noticed two tanned young men in cut-off jeans, waiting for the court. They were laughing with his wife. She was massaging her throat with lotion, like an actress out of *Sluts in Heat*.

"Hurry up and serve, Brian."

If I overpower their boy David with my hardest serve, I will look like a Fascist to Tracey, and it may not go in. If I hit him a soft serve, I will look like Chamberlain, an appeasing fool, and I might get blasted in the head again.

On both serves Brian forgot Stan Smith's advice.

"Two-five."

Threatening David with his racquet, Marvin shouted: "We're only one service break down."

David squeezed the ball he had retrieved, thinking, another game to lose.

The score quickly reached thirty-all.

"Don't call my shot out until it's landed!"

"My backhand's anorexic."

"Deuce."

"At least hit the top half of the net!"

"Unreal. UN-real."

"Deuce!"

"That was my shot!"

"My racquet's lousy. It can't hit overheads."

"Deuce again!"

"Who put that net there?"

The final game, and set, ended with a lofted ball that both father and son chased. David slam-danced Marvin into the cement, and Brian patted Nancy on her bottom in congratulations.

Marvin was up in an instant, claiming his friend's patting was, in fact, groping, which constituted wife abuse, and therefore the set was forfeited.

Stunned at this desperate ploy, Brian found himself saying, "We must do this again tomorrow."

Nanaimo, France

Was it fair Ken was now living and working in a town that was really an overgrown pulp mill? An exquisite torture after a big city like Vancouver, but, in other respects, less of a hassle, and after two years of under- and unemployment, he was grateful for any design work. And how could he complain when he now had enough money (at the current exchange rate of better than four francs for a Canadian dollar) to take his first trip to Paris?

Unfortunately, he would be jet-lagged, dragging himself in an irritated daze through his first hours in France, wasting precious moments in a country his imagination had long seen as marvellous. Only nine hours difference between these boxcar houses clad in grey plastic siding and Paris, but the ninety-three million miles between the earth and the sun felt less distant. For nearly a month, Ken had been designing a large-scale condo to fit inside the developer's mingy numbers—forced to create one more mausoleum—while he imagined the Eiffel Tower growing like a rose bush into the sky.

The developer had it stuck in the mind beneath his gelled black-dyed hair that not sawing up eight-foot sheets of plywood for the perimeter walls of each unit would mean big savings in construction. And in that squashed layout, this man who wore white pants, white shoes, and a white belt demanded a second bathroom. ("Everyone loves *en suites*, and you can't have guests traipsing through your bedroom to take a dump.") The purchase price had to stay below $75,000, so there was no breathing room.

All afternoon the stench from the mill at Harmac had drifted through Ken's window. The end of an unproductive day. His stomach growled, but he was *beaucoup* more ready for alcohol than food.

He pushed himself up from the computer and walked the six steps to the kitchen nook. There, next to the French phrase book, stood the half-empty bottle of Beaujolais. As he was tugging out the cork, Ken had an *illumination*: What if he lived his last Nanaimo week in the Paris time zone? That way he would arrive in France perfectly accommodated.

All he would have to do for the next seven days was wake up here on Vancouver Island at ten o'clock in the evening, have a coffee and croissant, then work on finishing the details for the tiny 1BR + 2BATH units. (The same size as some Paris apartments?)

But he would be trapped in this small rental "view" apartment, chest tight, staring out at the dark sea, looking into the heavy blackness of the Mainland where his life with Karen had once been located. He still wanted her to understand his need to go to Nanaimo and his wish to go to Paris. With a flick of her cinnamon hair, she had told him she was too busy for both. As he was leaving for Nanaimo, she had rolled and lifted her shoulders, her arms stretched out like wings.

The glass of Beaujolais had somehow evaporated.

The Hub City—people gave Nanaimo this name because lots of ferry traffic passed through. And it *was* vaguely near the geographical and population centre of the Island. Occasionally someone like Timothy Findley would read at the Bookstore on Bastion Street. There were a few reasons for people to come here from the even smaller places, logging camps and fishing villages, like Ladysmith, Port McNeill, and Ucluelet. Those who wanted a slightly enlarged life might settle for a tiny condo in the Hub City and help Ken fly to Paris.

"Architect Designed," the brochures and billboards would boast. He was doing his best work, but feared the drawings translated off the page would look like a dog's breakfast.

In his apartment were a few clumps of broccoli, a hardened end of cheddar cheese, and some out-of-date eggs. With such tight-assed specs, two bathrooms just took up too much space. No wonder the French ignored them, banished them, Karen had once told him, to the end of the corridor, leaving the interiors of Paris apartments *élégant*. Ken flinched at the idea of having his name associated with a nearly unliveable place.

The first time he had been aware of having drawn

136

anything well, his teacher had to remind him to sign his name. Ken had been barely conscious of his hands grabbing crayons. His eyes hardly looked at the wide paper, so intensely were they pulling in the steam locomotive, bright-black in the afternoon light. His hand had transferred its low triangular cow-catcher in front, the long, rounded belly with the high, fluted smoke-stack above, and those driving wheels in the Vancouver waterside park, motionless. He and the locomotive had come to a point of rest.

A piercing cry startled Ken out of his mesmerized looking. Turning his head sideways, he had seen the teacher, Miss Duncan, holding her sandals by their long straps, and he had thought she must have stepped on some broken glass. But he couldn't see any blood on her broad bare feet. The skin appeared smoothed around her eyes as she stared down at his coloured sheet of paper on the sidewalk. Finally, he realized it had been a shout of surprised pleasure at what had taken form on his wide, sunny page. For better or worse, that pure cry still rippled in his consciousness.

Ken decided to cut off the mould and make a broccoli *soufflé*.

He remembered being scared by Miss Duncan's different voice so suddenly exposed, like a white bum. There'd be no admiring cries for Arbutus Winds, where only two trees were left on the bulldozed site for cosy condominiums, where unit owner and guest could pee at the same time in different rooms. Dumb of him to want to hear that unbidden cry of praise again, unfair to expect it from Karen.

As a kid in the park that day—feeling more than seeing—Ken had been scared to pause, pressing down crayons against the cement until the train was in two places completely. In perfect proportion. Ken had saved the gold numerals until the end (like the painter of the three-dimensional locomotive must have), sensing the magic of numbers to pull trains all the way across a huge continent and through the Rockies to Vancouver, to the sea's edge where a small boy sprawled on warm spongy grass had drawn the steel circles with their connecting horizontal bars, perfectly still.

He chopped out the yellow-brown florets.

Miss Duncan had told him not to print, but to write out his signature (*Kenjones*), and had then inscribed his sheet with an "O," for outstanding. The grade had pleased him, yet, beside the train's true shape, it had felt strangely disfiguring.

As he walked home from the bus, he'd been caught in a sudden shower. He hugged the wide paper close to his chest and wondered if his mother would notice that the picture was special. The damp curve of coloured waxes must have taken on a near cylindrical form, like the rounded metal encasing the steam engine. Ken remembered her stretching it out on the dining room table, nodding once, then sliding his locomotive into the bottom drawer of the walnut china cabinet, under some purple place mats.

Those huge steel wheels must have been taller than he was then. A matter of perspective.

After years of staring at representations in photographs and films, what would the actual buildings of Paris look like to him? Not, he hoped, as familiar as broccoli.

He could pretend his *soufflé* was a very early breakfast, *son petit déjeuner*. At seven p.m. in Nanaimo, it

138

was already four in the morning in Paris. He didn't want to yawn his way through the Louvre next week, or drift past the palpable beauty of Paris buildings like a somnambulist. In Nanaimo there were some interesting structures, like the elevated octagonal wooden fort, and the red-brick Great National Land Bldg., with little set-back and its four splendid columns forming part of a curving face that rounded off the vee where the streets of Chapel and Church met, and maybe the windowless clubhouse of the Hell's Angels with its rumours of a severed head.

He flipped it half-over, then scraped it onto a plate. *Et voila!* With grey clouds in the Nanaimo sky, the red wine in the curve of his glass had to signify the sunset. Which was almost the same colour as the dawn, *l'aube.*

After a summer in France, Karen had come back to school speaking French phrases and wearing a moss-green sweater from the Champs-Elysées. In his first Biology class, while half of the rugby team wanted him to outline their microscopic cross-sections of a worm, Ken had been distracted by Karen's breasts: the woollen ribs of her sweater stretched like his breathing. In the next class she had handed him a huge stone, warning him of its heaviness. The airy pockets of lightness in the pumice had surprised Ken, and, lifting the rock high above his head, he had for the first time as an uptight adolescent felt good about laughing at himself.

He dropped the greasy plate into the sink. He couldn't imagine staying up for another hour, let alone staying awake for an entire night. In a mill town it was a pointless gesture to step outside for a breath of fresh air. Holding the stem sideways, touching the glass to his lips, and sticking out his tongue to taste another drop of wine, Ken imagined himself in Paris.

The restaurant, with its unappetizing name, "Filthy McNasty's," seemed close enough to what he thought a French bistro might look like: cut flowers, a bearded man scribbling, and soup-bowls steaming with flavours.

The waitress, in a cable-stitched sweater, walked towards his table, a jewel the colour of Beaujolais in her nose.

"*Café au lait.*"

"You want a *latté?*"

"No, a *café au lait.* There's no difference except for the foam."

"Do you think Quebec will separate? I think they should."

"No and no." How had he got into this conversation so fast?

She opened her mouth, "Will that be all? A dessert?"

Karen usually ate dessert while standing up talking on the phone to some client or agent about a house price, bumping her hip softly against the kitchen counter. She would drag her pink tongue along the edge of the spoon.

"*Non, merci,*" Ken said, wondering how his dream vision of France fitted in with his feelings about his own country falling in two. Splitting up was an ugly L-shaped room where a voice yelled around a right-angled corner to the opposite end at another who had stopped listening long ago. And because the sound had to ricochet off the walls before reaching someone, her, there might be nobody there when you finally cared

140

to hear someone else's voice instead of this stupid, tired one in your head that kept coming back, muffled and angled, and accusing.

The waitress placed his *café au lait* in front of him.

"*Merci beaucoup*. I'm going to Paris next week."

"I just got back from Mexico. I want to go again, as soon as I can save enough money, but I'm staying longer next time."

The waitress left him for another table, full of her future, and he remembered how in high school he had already known he had wanted to be an architect. Had dreamed of drawing shapely, measured lines on creamy-thick paper that was a pleasure to rub between thumb and forefinger, had imagined his inked shapes enlarged and repeated as glass, brick, wood, and steel to occupy a chunk of the world's sky as heavy, touchable objects— reversing the direction from that solid train engine to his sketchy copy on warm paper.

By the window, three young women, wearing mostly black, were loudly discussing a film. Probably students from Malaspina University-College, where wooden sheds and barn shapes, mixed up with PoMo clichés of concrete and glass, were thrown against the hillside. A jumbled burlesque of the bucolic and the urban. But made tolerable by the naive green of parallel awnings that gave the eye some giant steps between the ocean and the mountain ridge. These women with close-cropped heads were talking about a film, *Ready to Wear*, and seemed intent on creating a new idea of themselves. Here in Nanaimo, they were making up lives that perhaps weren't locatable in the tiny towns where they might have started. The exact opposite of himself? What had Karen said to him when he had phoned a month ago from the ferry terminal? ("Ken, *merde*, you have no leisure from self-concern.") One woman, mostly listening, had cupped both her hands around the clear bowl of her wine glass, her pale forearms pressed into a long, delicate stem, like a second wine glass. Ken wondered if the romance of faces never seen before had to do with a desire for a different one above your own shoulders. *Prêt-à-porter.*

The waitress brought the bill, then leaned her freckled face close to look at his napkin, "Where's that?"

Ken shrugged, "It's the Opera House, in Paris." An image of an image of a place he'd never seen. That Karen had. *Magnifique*, he hoped.

Heavy with fatigue, Ken rested against the door jamb of the Anza Club. It had to be a place for homesick Australians and New Zealanders, and, because his father had gone to Melbourne Grammar School, Ken hoped he would be welcomed. A burly man opened the door, a white scar curving down into his upper lip. He stared at the top of Ken's head. He looked like an older, meaner version of Franco, the school bully Ken had once pacified by drawing a fantastical car with speed lines racing into a future neither of them knew.

From inside the Anza Club came an angry voice, followed by someone's loud laugh, then the snap and flutter of cards. Ken raised a hand to brush at his hair, "Can I come in?" Still avoiding Ken's eyes, the doorman patted his breast pocket twice: "It's a private club. You need a thousand bucks to get in." More than Ken's whole budget for Paris. Would a red-inked drawing of a Ferrari do? The solid door swung towards his face.

C'était très impoli.

He no longer had enough electricity in his brain to pursue the adventures of a Nanaimo night.

Yet somehow here he was, still awake, jingling his car keys, walking under a white half-moon that had scooted free from massed clouds. Between some squat buildings, a man with a pony-tail was pissing against a blue dumpster while holding a shiny trumpet behind his back. After zipping up, the stranger turned quickly, then disappeared, almost below the pavement. Ken followed, stepping from the paved edge into a cool, endless basement which had a low ceiling held up by chunky posts of squared-off concrete. By the rectangular orange glow coming through the wire cages of plug-in heaters, he could make out jazz posters, and, against the far wall, stacks of *Down Beat*. Ken had somehow managed to find the Club Kolo Paradise Pacific. A young guy with a tight wool cap began playing a melancholy soprano sax solo.

Waiting in the shadows, smoke stinging his eyes, ears full of beautifully sad metal notes, Ken couldn't read his watch and felt contented. *Heureux. Comme un poisson dans l'eau.* It was like hearing the CD he had of Sidney Bechet playing in Paris exile, live.

Driving south on the Island Highway, through the light rain, Ken headed towards the high smokestacks of Harmac. A red rose he had bought lay beside him on the passenger seat. Just after the cut-off to Cedar, near the Bighouse, the pounding in his brain became so loud he needed to stop the car. He couldn't tell if this thick pulsing in his skull came from the wine and coffee in his bloodstream, or from the jazz session, or from Natives inside the Bighouse drumming and dancing their way through a long night. Did a place's feeling of largeness come from these unknowable lives in unentered buildings? In Paris, it was already after lunch, and people might just now be going for a leisurely walk through the Jardin des Tuileries, breathing in *toutes les belles fleurs*.

Fighting off dreams of sleep, Ken drove on, steering to the bend of the painted line. The road to Duke Point was empty. *C'était curieux*: near the mill itself, there was no industrial smell. He was breathing in clean air, *l'air frais*.

At the Harmac gate he could see bodies twisting, moving with machines in the night, building a city out of pulp, paying his wages.

Coming back through downtown Nanaimo, Ken could sense himself drifting off. He jerked the wheel and saw a woman in a lemon top, pink shorts, and red high heels standing under a corner lamp, hitchhiking. He stopped the car, leaned over, and rolled down the far window. He watched *la prostituée* walk over to his car. Her face chubby with innocence. In a dumb movie gesture, he snatched up the long-stemmed rose and held it out for her.

She took the red flower in both hands at once, and kissed the petals as if they were an open mouth. He was completely bowled over by her beautiful gesture. A cry ripped from his lungs. *Complètement bouleversé par ce beau geste-là!*

A man wearing jeans and running shoes and clutching a cell phone stepped off the sidewalk and glared. But Ken felt ragged with joy at her beautiful gesture, and it was only as he sped off, with cool air rushing through the open window, that his heart sank at the thought of what she had to do *pour gagner sa vie.*

Near the ocean, beneath the lightening grey sky, he stopped the car. He got out and gazed at the dim forms of boxcars, tankers, and flatbeds shunting in Johnson Terminal, banging together. Under the man-made lights, the suspended dust of their colliding looked like pale smoke. Ken leaned on the car's damp hood and looked at the ocean. A faint print of moonlight unrolled on top of the shifting sea.

Lumber, coal, salmon—not lovers—were about to depart. Yet, for Ken, this scene had lyric echoes of a film farewell in a French train station. *Toujours la tristesse.*

Back at his apartment, he glanced down at his printout. *Accommodations.* The lines of his condo design looked usable, and not totally inelegant.

Outside the window, *l'aube et les oiseaux.* The morning sky coloured the feathers of the gliding gulls a soft rose. *Il adorait ça.* He picked up the phone and gently pressed down the familiar sequence of numbers. *Toujours avec le matin venait l'espoir.*

"Hello."

Like finding billions of unknown pockets of air. *"Bonjour.* It's Ken."

"Merde. What time is it?"

"Karen, I'm sorry. I've just had a great sleepless night. Sight-seeing."

"It's six in the morning! Where the hell are you calling from?"

He could feel his pulse spurt. *"Paris."*

145

Colour Bodies

Running now past metal frames in dark greyness to the room's end wall where I lift a chrome bowl off a cold skull and pop the wire from the scalp and lug a like-bodied self towards the open door and the blue light switch and just hurry up but her feet drag and faster and dopple-dopple-dopplegänger and flop it up onto the waiting tray and it's me was me is was is me and talking to myself when I need to shut the open door and close out the light and changing and tangling gowns and tearing and I can't annihilate something that's nothing so I run and bump and grope my way back to the newly empty bed and try to become just a clone again because I will be nothing and nothing if S.A.W. finds out and I Reisa Bakhtin forgot to attach its wire and must once more race through charcoal air towards the door where my hands feel at a cold head like mine and I pop the wire onto its brain and shove the B.I.G.G. cap down to its ears and return past rows of white teeth to stick the wire back into my own brain and pull on the chrome hood to hide the shaven circle on my icing head and am waiting and why did Ruth feed me soup and it's not alive and just a nought and what did Yusef mean when he said he loved Lisa and I'm here and alive but I want to save my shadow self so I unstick myself again and get off the freezing tray and rush to the doorway where I flick on the big blue switch and she has a face that is mine with ice crystals on her brows and staring pear-green eyes that make me look away from its gaze towards a narrow inner door that opens to show a mop and a bucket and a folded blanket on a wide shelf and maybe the nurses won't look in there so I twist and lift and slide and heave the chilled body up there and wrap it in the heavy red squares of wool with the braided fringe tickling my lips before I slam the cupboard door and flick off the light and hurry back into my prone position and wait and wait for the AtGo rebels to rescue me having tried to save it when a knock sounds in my ears which I cover trying to warm my cold lobes but dreading the searing whoosh of vaporizing bone that left Ruth's blue gold ring to enclose nothing but transparency or earth so I feign sleep but there is again knocking from the closet by someone like me who is my base pair and only a shadow's shadow

As soft ice in a steel tray next to a shut door, I feel no pulse, and all this grey time is one numb length.

I want to end what has no start.

Though next in line, I am stuck here, with a wire in my scalp.

And I ache to thaw.

This blank form I share twice, thrice, more, in a cold room which holds too much nought.

Want not to be *next*, but out there, and taste warmth in my throat.

Not just be cells of near ice in one vast cold cell.

A dream I can't wake up . . .

Sharp light swings in with the door, and one of the ones in a white coat steps on the bright wedge of floor, flicks a big blue switch up, comes to the side of my steel bed, and eyes that glow wide stare down at me— so long my head hurts—and in my chest a great tight gulp shapes and holds the soft word: (yes).

A red pulse stings at my wrist.

These strange lips loom close, and I can hear a hot scent of air push out.

My heart pumps so loud my bones rock to its beat.

To the sound of wet pops, this one in a white coat snaps free the wire to my brain.

Warm quick hands jerk at my flesh, tilt my head so the room goes wrong, pull my new weight up, shake me right out of the cold tray—twist, lift, slide, slump— dump me on a flat thing with wheels.

And I ride out from my safe place by the wall, my skin wet.

Wheeled too quick past the swung door, and, yes, it's me (the next one) out in the hot light and this air too rich to take in, which clogs my nose, my mouth— hurts my new eyes.

I choke on all these first smells: salt, weeds, and blood.

∞

The one in white has shoved me through to time. With each new breath, sweet damp hay, and grease, cling to my brain.

A chunk of light falls out of the high grey air. The wheels hum and hiss.

Greens, blues, reds scratch at my face. While my tongue grows soft and large in my mouth.

The taste of tar and damp fur curls in my nose. Burnt gas, milk, shit, and wet seeds.

Bits of wet sky start to bounce off my new skin. My tongue turns and turns, tries to shape noise right.

"Thaw." A warm, damp hand on my lips stills my first word.

Taste lime. When the hand slides off, I see pink lines in its pale brown palm.

My lips try once more to push out clear sounds. Wet hits at—melts—my mouth.

The pale green eyes of this one in white blink shut. Its face now a sheen of rain as I'm wheeled fast down a long stone path.

Two lines of tall trees that want to join at a far point my eyes can't quite get to. My ice face warms and chills.

Near a huge tree we twist, jolt from the wide hard path. And it's a down and down rush to a dark shed with no doors.

Lines of black rain splash from the roof. And for the first time I flinch at the cold of cold.

The one in white bends, close. Bright bits of rain stick to its hair, and I want to cry out.

149

The hand with its small blue gold hoop goes past my face, feels at the dark stone wall. And all at once a slit grows wide—and now is a door the width of my damp hips.

A lurch, bump, and I'm in a small room that smells of burnt logs, and pear. The boom, boom in my chest I can't stop as hot breaths spill from my mouth.

Pale green eyes push on mine. "Pair" sounds in my head—the same way as its near word, "pear"—while the one in white spins and walks out.

My gut grabs tight, and once more I wait on my back, but this time not as blank ice: I am wet with the world. And breathe in the scent of fruit and ash.

I twist my stiff neck and watch the curves of two pale green pears bend the room's weak light. Their sweet forms tug at my eyes.

Lift my arm—that turns to flesh—and strain for them, for what is not me. But those green shapes mock my wish to bring near, to hold close, to take in.

Too much work and my arm thuds down through the dust which floats. A dead weight hits on my chest, where I now feel what must be pain.

Scrunch shut my eyes to close out what is too far to get. But my brain still glows, tart and bright with pears.

In my head I look at sharp light flow through veins on green skin. A rush of rain, and I look out of my eyes once more, see the one in white with slick black hair.

Its hand with the blue gold ring holds a clump of small disks. In the palm of the right, small tubes gleam.

The one in white glides by me, past the two pears, to where a thin steel rod—whoosh!—rains down in a cup I can see through. The discs and tubes fall in the air, sink slow in the glass, and the small blues, round greens, and long reds sink wet and flip, huff out specks of air.

At the brim a few weak snaps, and I nose the tang of fruits gone sour. A clear curve tilts at my face, as if I should know what to do next.

The hard glass edge thrust at my tense lips. Wet fizz thrown down my throat.

I choke, choke. Frost in my lungs.

The one in white slaps my back. Fierce tears squeeze from my eyes.

It pats dry my face with a rough sleeve, and snot gleams on its white coat. It props up my head, strokes my brow, but I close my jaw tight.

At last, the one in white sets down the glass cup. In the gap of its red, red lips, white teeth shine as it speaks out a word, "wet."

My teeth, lips, tongue, throat, lungs, try to shape the sounds back, but I hear my voice say, "wed." And part of its hand dips in the glass, slips moist past the skin of my lips.

Hurls the pills down my throat. I gag, and stare at the one in white who now swirls my hair, who feels near the top of my skull, whose sharp nail digs a small, round groove in my scalp.

∞

I wake to find no one. The pears, plump and pale green, are gone. Here is a strange new place where a fly crawls back and forth on a wide pane of glass. Its wings move free, but the fly hits with a bash what it can't get through.

On the far side of the flat glass are green shoots and stems with bright blooms. I swing a leg straight out. When it folds at the knee, my toes touch cold wood. I jerk my leg up. A voice from the next room shouts, "I'm not a Nazi!"

A mad buzz—ping!—as the fly hits the glass wall. (*Not* zee?) I wait for more words, or sounds. But just the beat, beat of blood in my brain.

I stick out my leg once more. Let it drop through the air. I push up and—for the first time—stand. Sway, as a high voice yells, "It's only a clone, Yusef."

My hand grabs out for the bed. Which starts to roll. And I bang down on the hard squares of floor. In the hush my nose sniffs and sniffs.

On all fours, I think of "pain" and "pane." A cry cuts through the wall: "I only want my memory back!" I freeze, then crawl fast, stretch high, squeeze a flap of cloth, tug up by the bed frame, and sprawl down on the sheet. A door clicks, and a plump one in a white coat with a mauve scarf on its neck and a blue gold ring in its black ear looks at me, sucks in its cheeks, and walks out.

The sprouts of hair at the big ends of my arms rub stink and slip, like ice that warms. On the far side of the wide glass, wind blows on the green plants and past the green shrubs and by the broad green leaves of a tree, and I watch the large dark head with its bright ring grow small, then move out of the frame I can see through. A loud moan comes from the next room. Quick breaths push from my mouth, while my lungs fall and rise.

My ears wait. At the next deep moan I step down and stand up. I slide, and slide, next, the next slide, now three fast nexts. Dare I lift a foot in the blank air?

Risk it, and find I can move like one who lives. Get to the door with the dull brass knob I can lean on. Push, lift, shove, twist, and I fall back as the fly in a quick buzz of wings goes out in the warm wide gap of day I have let in. Thick dust from plants wafts sweet stink scents up my nose.

On part of the lawn, shade and sun make the flat dark form of a tree. I step out and go blind. Squint, start to run in a hot craze of on and on. With each blade of grass I press down, my soles itch.

In front of me a bird with a red breast skies up to perch on the high wire fence as I fall. Face in moist grass, and my skin hot. I turn, see soft green on the tips of pine boughs, a wax green on some small plants that give back the light, and a pale green where wood stems out to make a new leaf, and near the buds, a thin green white skin. On my hand crawls a red bug with black dots.

It flies off as I rise up, next to a mound of wild green sprays. Warm gusts rock me. A fat bee with stripes of gold and black, and thick goo stuck to its legs, zings from bloom to pink bloom. On my skin I feel sharp dents from the blades of grass.

I scratch at my chest, and hear a cry of pure hurt that is not mine. From the brick house, in a box of glass that juts out to this whorl of green. See two tense curves. Watch a bone jab at flesh.

And a deep ache scoops me out. Down on all fours. I can't look, can't look, and look at how it wounds it. Flails at the air as if it wants to fly.

A sweet stench of blooms in my head. My eyes pulse and jerk. The red bug with black dots crawls through my brain. And where my legs meet, this wet heat.

In the box of glass, one that lies on its back turns its head and looks out at me. With a flash of bare legs leaps out of view, and now this form runs out on the lawn: straight at me. The hard dark eyes of her breasts stand out. Like short stems on two pears of flesh.

No wound gapes from the bone jabs to the flesh. But on her thigh, a white splash. I look up at this first face, then down, feel eyes watch me watch my own pale brown breasts. My skin, in both shade and sun, cold and hot at the same time.

Her hand with the blue gold ring grabs my soft arm. Yanks me to the door with the dull brass knob. And all at once I am back in this room where she bends my arm, and fists my hand. Her arm, which is just like mine, just like mine, lifts, sticks sharp steel in a round blue line of my flesh.

I wake to this cold new place (the fourth?), where harsh light hums. Like that first room of ice, wires, and steel trays. But no one else here. The faint scent of hurt flesh. On the far wall, a line of green light glides on a wide screen. I could freeze, held down by this chest strap and tight foot clamps. Look way up. See arms that hang down, and strips of meat on white bones.

Can't shove my eyes shut. Want back to blank ice form. But not like those arms that reach down from hooks in the roof. Their hands seem to want to touch my face. Chunks of ice stuck to numb parts which once felt life. Blotched now with cold red. Some with *no* hands. What will they slice off me?

The slab of square door scrapes, and my arms twitch. Two ones in white come at me. I squirm and twist, block the air in my lungs, but can't sit up. My ribs and shins fix me here. One is the dark one who wears the mauve scarf, and that blue gold ring in his ear. And a pale tall one with no hair on his head, who draws out a thin steel thing with a small hook. My hand, my lungs, my heart? I nose the warm mush I lie on.

Flinch and flex taut while the bald man drags the hook down the length of my left foot. Now sharp and slow on my right sole. The dark sad face stares at a round glass case that rests on his palm, his cheeks sucked in. The tall one lifts up a full tube with a long point and pricks my neck so hard my screams hurt my ears. At last pulls out the long steel end and holds up a blank tube in the room's cold air, next to an arm with fine blonde hair that sways on its hook. The warm touch of a dark hand at my wrist as I doze off. Where is that first one with soft green eyes?

Pears joined at their stems float round. They form chains that have no gap or end. And it is as if the pale green eyes of that first one in white glint in this dance of fruit. And I rise up with green veins in my flesh, and move in time. But when I look out from my head, I am still flat on my back, and just see a thin line of light flick on the far wall. Wires cross the floor, trail up the bed, and link to cold clips stuck to my head. And, in my brain, there's an itch that won't stop. The thought that if I look up I will see a part of my self on a hook.

By the thick door, a man with ice eyes. In a face that looks like a cold sun. He turns and goes out as the one who wears a mauve wool scarf comes in. The moist brown warmth of his eyes holds my gaze. He tongues his top lip and takes my hand in his. Too much flesh where he bows his chin. On his palm rests a glass case where small red blinks form, shift, and pulse past. He counts the strokes of my blood, and when he looks up once more, the wet gloss of his eye gives me back a small face.

The grey slab door swings in, then shuts, as the bald one with thin lips who now wears a clear mask on his eyes comes in, moves close. I glance up, see on a far hook an arm whose nails have pink paint. My line of green light leaps, and I want to tear the wires out of my scalp. The man with the mauve scarf lets go of my arm, taps at the round glass, at the flash, flash of my dots. His eyes blink, then he picks up a bright blade with a sharp, thin edge. I feel it press on my scalp—scrape—and red sounds scream out of my mouth. A clump of my hair now lies on the floor. Is that rain in his eyes?

I look up once more at those pink nails. My head fills with their mix of red and white. Blood and bones. Once more, a jab at my arm with a fine steel point. Head clips suck out my brain juice, and I slump on the soiled sheet. The sharp ups and downs on the screen change to round zigs and slow zags. Tied here, while the arm with pink paint spins in the breeze. The one with two full lips forms words out of the deep sounds in the neck beneath his scarf: "Not for Ruth, but Lisa, this maiming."

The bald one tears back the sheet, and my brain line flicks up on the screen. His mouth rolls in so there are no lips. The one with a blue gold ring in his ear tugs on clear gloves. From a small case he lifts out a grey rod with a sharp tip and puts its cold end near my face. Drags this cold wand up the nape of my neck and through the hair which I have left, and pulls this ice cold down past the brows of my eyes to freeze the whole length of my nose. A chill touch on my mouth, and, at last, the trail of ice slips off my cold chin. Frost on my lips. My head is split in two.

Do I numb or ache? Once felt the thaw of small cool rain: am I to chill back to nought? My cold head strapped down hard. The tall pale one tugs at a string on his mask that has its own nose and mouth shapes. He picks up a wide steel shaft. A tube with saw teeth that bloom at its end. As it turns, all the sharp points blur. Heat floods my crotch—a buzz like a world of crazed flies.

Its mean whir near my brain, where I can't watch, where I still try to match up names to things. Out there, pale green pears and eyes, her red red lips, that black slant of rain; in here, masks, thin lips, a mauve scarf, pink nails. And screams spurt hot out of all of me at the brute lurch of the drill that tears through the skin of my head. Grinds down through my skull. Foul smoke and hurt—and hurt, all hurt. My brain cells on fire. All dreams burnt out by pain. Too late, too late, when the drill lifts out, shuts off: hurt too bad for all my time.

A head that flares and scalds. My ice brain burns and burns. And from a hook, my bit of a friend hangs and twists. Did it choose that pink? Bright blood falls from my face, and drips down the edge of the bed frame. But can see both my hands on. Can still gulp down pure aches of air. My bum stuck shut, cold where my legs fork, and my throat raw from dry screams that won't stop.

My head ice fire hurt. In No Lip's glove a small, moist thing. Ice. Fire. Hurt. I can still name grey, white, red, as I drift. Out. A bit of my brain.

When I wake, my head flames with cold. And dim shapes throb, and rush by. Light beams suck up the black air. Trees stand out, one by one, as we slow for a curve. I breathe in salt, pine sap, kelp, the stale sweat of my skin, as the bald man turns the wheel this way or that, or not at all. A lone star hangs in the night. In my skull a hole of blank air. Dark blood sticks to my hand. I reach up to put out the fire in my head, and touch rough gauze on top of fine wire mesh.

The round bone of my head cored out. I stroke the patch of gauze, feel at the hard thin wires. When we pause here, can see in our lights rough bark on thick trunks. Where's my wet grey chunk with its white strings? Was in the cup of the hand which now jerks the wheel and steers down a steep night road. Now there's no glove on his hand blotched with my blood. He blows some short harsh word out through his teeth. Where's the flap of skin to glue me back down?

To clicks and jolts, and the scrape of a branch, I watch the star bounce in and out of the front curve of glass, and try to call to mind my "life." "Ice" . . . "green" . . . "nought" . . . "pear" . . . "pair" are some of the words left in what's left of my brain. I pick at the dried blood on my arm. But how can I scratch for what I might have known? We twist past a huge grey rock, and I smell marsh gas. How can a mind know of its own gap? On his sleeves thin blue stripes mark out blank space. His smooth skull I want to claw at, rip out his brain, heave it . . .

All at once, the trees are gone. Bare sand, the sea, and cries of gulls. We stop too fast, and my chest strains with tight breaths. High in the sky, out to sea, grey light and rose light brush, and mix—like blood on the earth's brain. He steps out. And a cool salt wind licks at the deep hole in my head. He shakes what I can't see. The sharp scent of his pee makes my nose itch.

A new day. My stiff limbs long for green grass and a gold sun. The bugs and buds and blooms and birds. No Lips climbs in, and there's a soft clunk as we start to whine back up a long curve. A turn and, there, once more, are the two lines of tall trees that want to join, but can't quite merge as one. Can't get rid of their gap. The van jolts off the road, rides on rocks, and bumps to a halt. I stare at the shed with no doors.

He tilts his head, waits, then gets out fast and slams some thing down in back. I'm wheeled out on a ramp in the soft light of dawn. His hand feels at the wall of stones, but can't find the right one to move since no chink shows. His thin lips hiss a word like wind through the pines. He strides past me, bends down, lifts up a black pot, takes out a key thick with rust. Some red brown dirt on his cuff as he fits the key in the wall of stones, and with a click lets the light in. He scoots me past the sill to where cold ash and two pears wait for me, and their twin plump shapes curve me back in time. My lips press down twice, stretch out, voice the word sounds of these pale green fruits that give me a time when I was whole.

His hands free my lungs from the strap, and when I rub at my squeezed breasts, he grins, says, "Base pairs."

From what's left of the store of words that a wire once fed to my brain, I pluck out "low," "first," and, "bass," but can fix no hard sense to his sounds, so I let "base" drift off in the room's damp air. "Pairs" as in "two twos," or "pears" as in "fruit," or "pares" as in "cut out a slice of your brain"? When he takes the clasps off my legs, I kick out at his hand. His thin lips roll in, and he tears back my sheet. His eye blink as if my cold skin from numb toes to my chilled aching head flared up too bright. He shrugs the sheet back on some of me.

Want to pierce his smooth head with a slow drill— bite a soft wet hunk of his live brain in two. I scrunch my scalp and can feel the wire mesh move. At a click I turn my head and see that first one in white. She stares down on me with big green eyes, asks, "What's it doing here?" No Lips bites at her ear lobe, says, "Chen felt it was too risky to keep among the cold cuts." I gaze at the pears that were once part of a live tree, at their stem ends which point now to blank space. "He has been paid in full; we'll drop it off when we do the insertion therapy." On her nails, pink paint glows.

My bit of a friend on a hook? She comes near in a wet grey dress, and a blue cap sewn with red birds, tugs the sheet up to my throat, speaks with ice in her voice, "I'm not prepared to be the *least* among Equals because of a dumb accident." She walks to the sink, makes rain spray out of a tap—sploosh!—the plonks caught in a round pan. The bald man jerks her tight, shoves his mouth at her neck. "You drank too many sex pheromones," she says, "let go." "At go," he drawls— his words a buzz of sounds that make no sense and ache in my head. Want her red lips to kiss the wound in my brain.

But she stands far off, as the pale man moves to a tall white box, swings out its high wide door, puts his hand in, and pulls out ice. His thin lips squirm while he mouths the hard chunks. She picks up a cup and shakes some green dust in. He yells at her, "We have to get rid of it before the nurses arrive." I press down on the gauze, and a moan falls out of my mouth. Her eyes look at mine, but when he makes a loud crunch in his mouth, turn back to him. "Yusef has quit AtGo. You can forget about your fruit chunking."

Pink nails fling up, and her voice pleads, "Tom, you promised to help." They have names, I ("it") do not. Tom, the male of birds and beasts, or one of low rank with a gun, and two toms is a drum to beat. Like my heart beats out my time, but at whose wish? The pink nails dip and are lost to view as she turns her back. "We can't do it without Yusef," Tom says. Her eyes damp as she brings the cup to me, lifts out a spoon of green broth. "Why bother to feed it now?" Tom shouts. She shrugs and smiles, squats, while my mouth lets in salt earth seeds that burst hot on my tongue: hurt and joy the same?

The spoon lifts to my slurps, and it's as if I take in moist soil that steams. The food slides in, past my burnt tongue, swirls down, but no spoon can fill the large hole in my skull. She raps the cup's hard lip, says to Tom, to No Lips, "Chen could be persuaded to assist us. In any case, the unused parts have to go back to the meat plant for recycling or disposal." Rage or fear chokes me, and when she tries to spoon more soup in, there's a sick surge in my throat. Green goo now on her coat. She wipes at it with the edge of my sheet, then walks to a small door in the wall which she pulls wide. Tom nips once more at the lobe of her ear. When I pinch my own ear lobe, a slight buzz down my spine, and a sore ear.

She takes out a long shape of grey cloth. Rests its huge soft mound of ridge and fold on her neck. Like a too big brain. Her real head hid. Then the birds on her cap take wing, sky up through the wide hole at the top of the dress that now falls smooth, down to her knees. For a blink of time her pale green eyes can't quite see where she is. By her nose stray long hairs hang limp and out of place. Just as *my* nose starts to twitch, she sweeps the strands in back of her left ear, in a dark curl, tells him, "I have official data on Chen's code violations I could leak to the nurses."

His teeth crunch down on his ice. "Ruth, you will owe me . . ." His arm with its striped cloth blocks my view of her face. "R-r-r-uth," I growl out. The red birds on her cap hop. She stares right at me, then her hand, with pink gloss on its nails, picks up one of the pears. She skins it with a knife, chops a piece out, tongues it off the blade, and chews. "When it's over, Tom, you'll get a dozen of my prize eggs to hatch out with your favourite sperms."

My mind lost. He walks to the fridge, swings out the high white door, and grabs at more chunks ("chunking?"). On the strewn ice, a small clear bag. I'm deaf to all but my own loud breath. Is that a cold bit of my brain? I slide off the bed. Race the whole width of the floor to clutch—soft!—at the chilled bag. This red, white, and grey thing, *mine*.

An arm bone pressed to my voice box. My bare feet dragged on the floor. Whose shrieks are these in my skull? My lungs two dead sacs. The bag of brain slips from my hand and hits with a plop. The hard arm slides off my throat. And I take in sore air. Gape, as Ruth scoops up the bruised blob of my mind.

She lays it back down on the ice, throws shut the fridge door. Feel a squish of moist pear flesh in my toes. My grey brain, a kind of cold fruit. Her eyes fix on mine, her face hard and still as ice. But now starts to shake. Her face now so wet I could drink there. Her cap flops off, and in the nest of her black hair, on the top left side of her head, there is a bald spot. The scalp skin like a pale brown egg.

∞

I am a copy of this woman who keeps me for her own cold use.

"Ruth," he says, to my double.

Like hundreds and hundreds of blades of grass pressed against my skin, the shape of her body printed on mine.

I tremble, and finger the criss-cross metal lines in my skull.

Again, he names her, "Ruth."

But "pity," "grief," "remorse"—the meanings I fetch from my drilled-out brain—do not suggest this selfish, hard woman.

His hand traces the curved length of her lifted arm (that is the very same as mine) from shoulder curve to muscle bulge to bone elbow to finger feathers, until Ruth's hand flickers, and the arm swoops down like a bird.

She whispers, "Pointless to go on," her eyes blurring.

The exposed flesh from the pear wet between my toes.

Ruth, both arms tight against her sides, sighs, "Instead of fixing my wonky neurons, the traumatized implant might do more damage."

One of his nails outlines the egg shaven into her long hair.

"Maybe not," he says.

The tip of Tom's index finger strokes Ruth's bald spot, and my own brain tingles.

"Ruth, I could scan the tissue for chunking damage after hours at the coroner's office or in Chen's lab."

I look towards the handle of the freezer door that is too far to dream of reaching again.

"Maybe he's butchered something new," Tom suggests.

"Chen only has legal access to brains with gross defects, which is not exactly what I need."

He nuzzles her like a bald bee at a flower, humming, "I'll help, I'll help," and fingers with pink nails caress his arched neck.

Their doubling, their two, makes me one nothing.

Is it lostness in my brain or a newness in this world that makes all things both vivid and blank?

Their kissing lips, through a weird suction of air and moisture and feeling, empty me out.

That plastic bag of myself in the freezer: dead or alive?

He renews the pressure on her (*my?*) lips, and I take one very quiet step.

Ruth unclasps him, "Later Tom," her pale-green eyes on her self-same flesh over here.

Can she know my thoughts as fast as they flit through my—*her*—cortex?

Frees herself from the clutch of his taut body, pivots smoothly away, and pulls a drawer open, and I have taken only one step closer.

Am I better or worse than all those chilled noughts that still wait frozen, never to be next—and how does "numb" relate to "number"?

Her shoes point this way, at her carbon copy.

Speaks to him, "We need to assay the neuron coring and remind Chen he can't thumb his nose at our deal."

Her pear breath warms my eyes.

Tom-toms in my chest, and a flashing needle—this piercing, the hollow point steeping my body in fatigue.

My head slumps, heavy and brainless.

$$\infty$$

Startled to life again, I'm in a grey gown. Watch an arm in blue stripes come out of a box coated with white ice-fuzz, bag again what has been taken from my head.

Ruth picks up her cap with its threaded birds and hides the egg shaved on her scalp. The sliver of my brain tissue hefted in his bony hand.

From a hook she snatches an orange cap with the letters "B.I.G.G." Covers my head in a perfect fit.

"The cap might fool the nurses for awhile if Safety and Wellness has been alerted." They push me outside, into wind and the light dark.

What does this mean, and what does "mean" mean: "intend" or "portend," or "cruel"—the "norm"? One word has become many confused sparks firing all at once inside my throbbing headbone as I'm rolled up into the van.

My eyes shut, and I listen to the same changing sounds of the engine. As my tired, drugged blood again floats me away to something like sleep, I wonder if the linking of words—or even a single one—can stretch over empty space, like steel mesh.

My eyes blink open to a double row of high grey-green trees that mark out the road. Their very straightness sends me back in time, to a restless rest.

I dream of green ice before Ruth's voice, low and listless, intrudes: "Once I had a perfect memory and now my brain can't re-learn the names of things I eat every day." Stopped under a full yellow moon.

"But am I ready to risk putting a defective blob in my head?" In a nearby field, a globe-eyed creature wears patches of both night and day, flicks at itself, and from its swollen bag hang tubes like long, soft-tipped fingers.

"I'll check it for damage first." We hurtle on, speeding somewhere beyond the creature's fenced life.

Tom's lipless face in the small mirror glued to the front windshield. And life-sized beside him, my own hateful image, Ruth.

She holds the small plastic bag of living tissue and cries. What's the matter with her brain matter?

I'm dozing to the thrumming engine as the van bangs to a halt, flings my body forward into a strap that cuts at my drowsy flesh. Bounces my dreaming head.

Outside, the ground and the trees have nothing left of green. The fields are shade, edged by an ashen sky.

And there's a cube building with two lights. The rush and clank of the van door sliding open.

Ruth, followed by Tom, strides towards the man who waits, his face partly turned. Ruth says something I can't hear to the moon-coloured face.

He shakes his head, and she jams a thumb up his nose, pinches, and twists. When she pulls her hand away, Chen (it must be) takes the small bag of brain fragment from Tom.

They all enter the squat building, between the winking amber lights. And I thrash against nylon belts until I'm tired and hurt, then slump into sleep.

Ruth wrenches the van's door wide, frees me from the chrome buckles and straps, and her eyes slide all over her face. She heaves me upright beside her in the night, and starts to drag me towards the concrete structure when, all of a sudden, the sky is being sliced up.

∞

The hard shell of the van rattles. And the huge beating noise above sets off a matching loudness down in my chest. The slashing thing falls in a shudder rhythm. Flings dirt at us, seed pods, and sticks, as Ruth shouts, "The nurses."

A clear giant egg with metal rails. An object beyond my naming. Must be missing the neurons for its word—that slice, slice. Figures in gleaming pale-blue helmets, large shoulder pads, and bone-white shirts run out.

They point flared things at the two of us. On their helmets are silver zig-zags, like sharp teeth. Chest-high red squiggles form three letters, "S.A.W." One nurse snaps a tight pair of linked bracelets around my wrists and shrieks through a face shield, "I've captured Ruth Perez."

Only her sister flesh, or semblance, shadow, brain source, mirror, and daughter. The same nurse jabs the hard weapon between my ribs. Prods me doubly with its flared steel end. The nasal voice squeaks through the solid visor: "Your cap signifies you to be a member of The Board in Genome Governancing."

Only a scared copy. "Confirm you are Ruth Perez." No, hundreds like me, frozen in metal trays, filed row after row, waiting for a lifetime. But these nurses believe I am more than an echo.

A sucking whoosh, a huge bang, and black smoke billows up as the cubed building crashes in on itself. The meat plant, with its thick concrete walls, has imploded. Thrust down in a mass of rubble and grey dust that settles in the cloudy night. Next to this trembling pile of debris, the pair of us wait.

Guarded by burly nurses in high white boots. No sign of Tom, the tall, bald, lipless man with the blurring drill. Must be torn apart and flattened, along with Chen. And my stolen brain cells.

A gleaming weapon swings up into my eyes, and I stare into a hollow tube and want *not* to be next. A nurse wheels over a low compact machine with turquoise wires, silver leads, and zig-zag red decals. Its dial needles to zero. This nurse knocks Ruth's cap off, and I see—close to where the nurses attach a clip to Ruth's head—on the left side, in the middle, fairly close to the top, a piece of gauze where the egg spot *was*.

My tongue flutters, says nothing. A large nurse, the one with the most gleaming teeth on its painted helmet, yells at Ruth: "Confess you are only spare parts." This face, which is a perfect echo of mine, freezes. Now she is my true sister.

All their weapons swivel, point at the pale green eyes of my double. Ruth's breath goes and comes, noisy and urgent. Sniff-snort, sniff-snort, as the needle on the machine wings madly. My tongue darts in its dry mouth, but what words I whisper are too quiet even for my ears.

My semblance mute. The head nurse props up Ruth's chin with a thumb knuckle: "We require your voice print, now." A funk of terror sifts from her flesh to mine. Black hair like hers tangles in front of my eyes.

A name, Bogdhan, sewn into the back of the kevlar coat worn by S.A.W.'s head nurse. He tears off his chin strap which swings back and forth in the moonlight like the sensor needle. Always too late to wish for what's gone, a safe shadow life on ice. He gestures to the large dome that rests on the stretched curled rods, and gloved hands shove at me—propel the pair of us into the huge bubble of scentless air just below three long whirling blades.

A see-through egg whose clear curves wall us in. And I see my double look at her other double, the one who bends on the glassy wall. Two cold circles of metal splice her hands too, and I observe my own echo self that's splayed open on the concave glass in front of my eyes. Counting both our images, we make a pair of glum pairs.

To the racket of ten van engines, we vibrate and climb straight up, the blades cutting the harmless air. Now lean into the sky, but can't watch where we're going because my curved image gets in the way, and even the thick visors of the nurses repeat, make small, darken, mis-shape, slice up, and return to me this borrowed face of mine. Zippers slide on jackets, chin straps pop off, visors unclick, and the moon shows the naked, nearly human faces of the nurses: Bogdhan, Ying, Chico, Elvis, and Nikki. Ruth still as ice as we shudder on.

A quick tilt, and we fall. Hover, before we lower to a noisy rest. Under a wind-storm of blades I'm pushed out onto a small paved square. The stench of wet earth in my nostrils. A sudden beacon glares in my eyes, and we begin to move in a single row, along a narrow wooden walkway.

The beacon goes dark. Bogdhan halts us, while wordless voices croak. A black mask without holes is pulled over Ruth's face. The high beacon pulses out a new signal just as blindness is stretched tight over my eyes.

One wrist is unclicked. Tugged forward by the lone handcuff, I shiver, listen to the boot-heels of the nurses thumping in a dead cadence. From out of the marsh stink come throated sounds that refuse to become words. And each of my steps in this double dark is like learning to walk without a world.

Can't trust the heavy rhythm of their marching. I bump against a rigid body. A sudden rattling as if a metal sheet were being rolled up in pieces, fast. My weighted bracelet yanked hard against the bone where my hand begins.

∞

Warm dry air when a nurse takes off my itchy blind-fold. Light cuts at my pupils. Elvis unsnaps the single handcuff. The nurses, a swivel of masks, crowd around us, waving their flared guns back and forth between me and Ruth. As I press at my sore wrist-bone, Nikki knocks my cap off. I ponder the letters on the floor: B.I.G.G. "Which one is she?" Nikki rips the blood-rust gauze from my sister's skull.

Ruth's face zigzags. Her skull only hollowed out, so there was no time to insert my brain slice. Elvis leans over, tears the strip of gauze from my head—hurts, still hurts—peers through the wire mesh at my absence. "Both have a hole scooped out of the left temporal parietal area." "Maybe Ruth Perez was going to assay the sample from the quarry against her own brain ore, or attempt an upgrade from the genomic library." "Which one is she?" No cross-wires under Ruth's bandage. "Prepare to attach the subjects for PET scanning and coding re Other Tests, Three and Nine, the Darwin and the Shelley."

They half-throw Ruth into a narrow doorway while I'm pulled backwards across the marble floor. Pushed now into a room shaped like a funnel, cinched to a large chair that's bolted to cement beside an iron and glass table which displays a shiny chain-saw. Wires slurp onto my skull, liquid spurts into my pierced arm, and my doped eyes watch a giant screen on the far wall pulse to brightness. A bag of skin flutters, billows, and, with a fierce snap, bloats tight, as a ship sails along the long wall's still surface through a spray of sea, but never reaches the curved corner where the room bends back to me. Two dirty gulls chase after a wooden ship. They fly across black lava, paired. Cones, sandstone, craters: an empty moonscape of islands. The two birds tilt in blank blue sky, swoop down to rest on waves beside a bobbing vessel, rocking next to its painted name, *Beagle*, their floating feathers ashen.

"A little world . . . found nowhere else." A hidden voice talks (to me?) in gaps. "First landing . . . the birds . . . strangers . . . tame . . . killed . . . stick." Is there a crater inside my cortex? No speaker I can see whose lips shape and reshape the air, only nurses with their mouths shut under visors. "A broken field . . . having been heated by noonday sun . . . sultry . . . little weeds . . . woods appear from distance quite leafless . . . black lava . . . an arctic." I try to cross over the barren hollows of the language, but sink into deep gulfs, fall into the huge crater between "sultry" and "arctic." Grasses, lushly green, stun my eyes, and for an instant I forget I am only staring at a filmy wall I can't see through.

An urge to seize the orange handle of the chainsaw and cut my way out. On-screen now, dead-centre, a lipped bowl upside down, ridged by shiny segments. Pebbly legs, a stretched neck, and an eye like a circle. A giant tortoise bites at grasses. And now a different tortoise with a shell "like a saddle" the voice says, that is scooped up to free the neck of this creature, which travels on longer legs over arid ground. If the second tortoise were stuck in a down-domed shell, it couldn't lift its head high enough to nibble on those cactus buds. From under this plant that a minute ago was ocean, the voice with no body intones: "Adapt or die."

Brine trickles down my brows into my eyeballs. As spike-backed sea lizards dive into icy water to feed on algae, then crawl out to bask on the black cliffs. "Hideous . . . sluggish" things, with clutching claws, weird tails, and dirty, rock-like heads. Stupid faces look into the sun as they stare out of the wall right at me. My head wants to slump away, but a metal chin-rest holds up its tired weight. Now from floor to ceiling shines a long white fleece of beard, and dark brows guard eyes which are both furtive and bold. My own eyes flutter, filled with the smooth, hairy strangeness of humans. And I voyage to a place near sleep.

But an ocean spills and thunders and froths. Tidal waves smash me down. Awake or dreaming, I fear death by drowning. My eyes can find no splash of water on my body. Undamp, I regard a filmic shore, filmic cliffs, filmic waves. This wet roar of breaking surf, only a dry image. And above the beaches, the rugged black masses of lava—despite their fissures and dark, narrow ridgings—are just the far flat wall wearing its wide, shifting mask. And now hoarse bellows as a giant tortoise digs in under a female's hard shell.

My watching self, a dreamer with eyes open. The flashing wall noisy with mating as I glimpse next to the chain-saw, a figure with a blue-gold earring and a mauve scarf who picks up a waste basket. He is gliding away, but my head can't turn, and my groggy eyes must follow a flight of finches into a sky that has become black lava. Yusef. My eyes try to turn backward. But they close instead, and I ride up a rocky beach on a huge bone saddle, my body dripping with arctic water as I cling to the welded plates of an immense tortoise which carries me onto a burning stone island where I am plunged into dirty, starless night. Headless, I now steer the shell of a van through endless grey-black sand. Its pair of dim lights reveal half-buried tortoise eggs lying unhatched in the heated sand, while in palm trees monkey torsos hang with pink nails and human faces.

A nurse shakes me (awake?), and I glimpse a garden of painful greenness, while fruit fragrance seeps into my nostrils through tubes with metal clips. The entire wall shines with an image of one like my self, but she is plumper, happy—*newer?* Stands beside a second being, and both these humans are so naked they don't even know they're naked. Idling by gorgeous flowers, as tame beasts cavort under soft pears that have no bruise. A quiver of life in his hanging parts. The female form smiles, as the coiled snake around her neck glistens. From its tortoise head darts a parched double tongue. The one with the shaky thing between his hairy legs talks to the vacant air, "Did [axons] I request thee Maker . . . to [dendrites] mould [cortex] me? Did [synapse] . . . I solicit thee [ions] from darkness to promote me?"

A nurse, Chico, stooped beside my elbow, twists the words louder by turning a purple dial. On the screen of the wall, or of my eyes, or of my brain, the sudden flash of a pale, lovely forehead that's shaped by sunny hair falling to bony shoulders in smooth, centred sweeps of brightness. This new-born image says she "should furnish . . . some account . . . of" how upon this idea of a monster "this dreaming girl" began "to dilate." Her voice rings like raindrops in an empty glass: "I lived on dreary shores, but it was an aerie of freedom, and I could commune with creatures of fancy." Numbers flick on a strip of light near my hand. On the wide wall a spectral man bends, tries to infuse a huge, ill-sewn creature with a brilliant spark. *Dreary night:* Behold the lifeless thing! Am I a creature of fancy?

The monster waits, just lies there on its back. *Candle nearly burnt.* Through window shutters the moon's *dim yellow light* colours the eyes of the one gazing down on the immense, formless body—he can't *endure the*

174

aspect of the *being* he has made. *Dull yellow eye opens; it breathes hard.* Giant limbs convulse. In a blink, horror and disgust push its maker out of the room and—breathless—down the stairs. *Watery eyes in sockets of dim-white* stare at me above *black* sealed *lips.* I scream and scream at its huge stitched head—at that monstrous *corpse* that breathes.

"Bogdhan, the arrow for clonal didn't flash." "The pulse read-outs imply her affect take-up was mainly funnelled through the maker, not via pity for the monster." The nurses remove my head clips. "Chico, contact Igloo to confirm missing tissue." ("Did [synapse] I solicit thee [ions] from darkness to promote me?") "Why would Perez, when she is Co-Chair of B.I.G.G., commit tissue fraud?" "Maybe to profit in spare parts?" Hostile eyes of the nurses turn on me, but they're nothing next to the creature's dead yellow ones in an immense green face.

"Elvis reports that test results next door for Subject 'B' are inconclusive." "Bogdhan, Igloo reports one empty tray." "If *this* subject is the primal Ruth Perez, despite some of her affect being attached to the monster. . ." "You monkey brain, Other Tests are designed to detect deep structure and are always shadowed." "Chico, you must have a hole in your cortex as big as both these two subjects if . . . " "Silence, give them Other Test Thirteen, the Gene Splice." The nurses scramble with clips and wiring, glomming suction cups back onto my sweating skin. "But, Bogdhan, sir, don't we require a permit for running this?"

"Run it under Hybrid Head Alarm." And I'm breathing in rotting fruit pulp, and watching small flies ascend and land on sagging pears. Clumped tight segments of a huge eye glisten, like an oval of flower buds. Now, on the far wall, the red sheen of the fruit-fly's eye transforms itself to whiteness, and "DEFECT" flashes in large black letters. *Two pairs* of wings extend from the *same* thorax, and a voice screeches: "Mutant genes!" Swampy air clogs my nose, and tadpoles waver, then swim frog-like into my eyes. Human fingers grasp dozens of needles, spurt sticky fluid over the slime of floating eggs. A nurse pierces me, injects yet one more drug into my punctured body. I watch a dwarf mouse get an extra gene, then view a great mammal bulk double and transmit its new germ-line for hundreds of images that flicker in giant sameness, while its lifted trunk wails in my skull and nurses measure my heartbeat, time my tears.

"Its affect is too strong for mere clonal status, even when controlling for a brief entry into human time." "Brain-wave patterns, breathing, pulse, and the psyche scan, all suggest Subject 'A' is *primal*." Tadpole sperms with flicking tails and bulbous heads collide and tangle. "Are you Perez?" In my silence I am ruthless. Oocytes mutate, age, and are shed into dry bowls. "Her sensate charge fulfills norms." "And hybrid testing can induce muteness, even without trauma from coring." Brainless.

"Elvis reports that the Gene Splice Test results for Subject 'B' were mixed." The nurses seem glum and puzzled beneath their pale-blue helmets. Ying scratches at the top of her hard helmet. Am I somehow beyond the wiring of their brains? The tiny alloy logos of chainsaws pinned on their jackets match the colours of the life-sized one on the table. "Maybe in trying to pass as *primal*, Subject 'B' began to mimic a living Equal."

Bogdhan nods, and Ying leans towards me, unties my gown. My smooth belly cooling under their gaze.

"Like Eve, no navel." Now Bogdhan is shouting into a piece of curved red plastic full of holes, "Elvis, scan Subject 'B' for umbilical link." Chico mutters, "Subject 'A' couldn't simulate that level of affect." Perhaps I *am* Ruth? No, just her mirrored flesh. "The problem is many Equals out of vanity ignore the Code, and get a plastic surgeon to graft skin over their belly buttons." Bogdhan's gloved fingers touch the flared weapon which dangles from his velcro belt. "Ying, contact B.I.G.G. Command and get a de-list order."

I glance upward, but no limbs hang from hooks. "Elvis reports Subject 'B' also has no navel." Am I to be given a life to live as long as I pretend to be Ruth Perez? "Bogdhan, B.I.G.G. Command requires a signed ink request slip." "Those off-springs of apes! Can't they compute my voice-print? Bogdhan Smith here, Leading Nurse, licence number seven hundred and twenty-two." I shiver, and wonder if Subject "B," waiting in the next lab, also trembles.

Nikki belches. "Sorry, my stomach can't handle these new rations." Bogdhan scowls at her. Speaks into the cup of holes that looks like a fruit-fly eye, upside down or inside out. "You plankton brain, refer to Standing Orders on Tissue Fraud, Chapter four, Section one. Thank you for granting an oral permit to take all needed steps to assess and secure a complex clonal breach." Then says under his breath, "It's like talking to a petri dish!" What would it feel like to have someone else's cells in my cortex?

"Ying, contact S.A.W. Central, and find out if another unit has adopted anyone else in the AtGo gang."

177

Nikki belches again, and there's some muffled barking. The nurses—and even Bogdhan—laugh at this sequence of sounds from a human to an unseen dog, their laughter a kind of echo of an echo. I start to laugh, but Bogdhan glares down at me. And I feel tears wet my laughter. Instead of a navel, a hole in my head. From where I pulled out the word "cortex," the covering of trees, and thought that laughter was a kind of human *bark*ing, which started in the "bark" of our brains. But my skullbone couldn't protect my cortex, didn't shelter the living neurons that made me up. "Bogdhan, at this point in time, there is no one else from AtGo staying at our Wellness Clinics."

"Bring in Subject 'B'." In this taking of brain matter, who is the first donor? "Subject 'A' wore the B.I.G.G. cap and must be Ruth Perez." Only her frozen shadow. Whose brain partly lets light fall in. Elvis prods Ruth into this room. The weapon's end, a hungry mouth. I look away from its gleaming metal, into her head's deep, airy gouge.

I'm uncinched, placed next to my living image. Sprayed now with the sudden noise of jacket zippers sliding shut, chin straps popped back into place, visors clacking down beneath pale-blue helmets. Their bootsoles scuff closer. To insist I'm clonal is to claim a nonself; to pose as Ruth Perez is to assert an unself. Like her, I wait. ("An oral permit to take all needed steps . . . .") The nurses ready to select, pick up, bite into, ingest one of us. The wall screen pulses, fades out. And Nikki's white boot whumps into Ruth's belly.

She moans like she did when Tom stabbed her middle with his bone thing. "Do you belong in the Igloo?" The vocal bark of Bogdhan's question sets off a dim echo from the dog, but this time there's no laughter.

The chain-saw on the table waits in stillness. Once was in mindless dream-time. "Testing has *confirmed* your clonedom." I know he lies to Ruth. But my lungs are squeezed too tight to pity the one who gave me my face.

"Who quarried your skull?" Bogdhan wants *her* to answer, but I nearly call out names like "Tom" and "Yusef" (and "Chen"?). Her pear-green eyes look at me, at this creature made without her sex organs—and made with her sex organs. The far wall glows on with fat silver shadows of swaying limbs. I'm a no-name. "Other Tests disclose that you have time lodes and living traces not permitted in mimic tissue." Ruth's lips don't open, and I nearly shout that they are barking up the wrong tree. "We will wipe your engrams clean."

Her lips form a silent red zero. Bogdhan barks a command: "Remove it to the asbestos wall." The nurses march Ruth across the marble floor to its metal edge and raise their guns up to their hard, clear visors as she stands alone in front of a whitish wall stained with charcoal. "Extinct the clone!" With a sucking pop her hair is in flames and weapons are melting away her face (*my face*). Foul smoke rushes the cells of Ruth's flesh through the open doorway and up my nostrils, to lodge in my cortex. Flecks of ash singe my hair as the pathways of my own brain feel on fire. Like billions of black suns, my neurons seem to spark and explode, but her pain beyond my knowing . . . here in this burnt air.

∞

Ruth disappearing in a tree-shaped fire, arms out like branches.

In this killing air I pant on, my tongue coated with bitter oxygen-fed ash—needing the very gas that helped burn her to stay alive.

Bubbles, hisses, and some last molecular twitches on the concrete floor where her hard bones melted.

I slump nauseated, in a surround of savage heat and loathing.

My self-same flesh disassembled.

Winds helically up in smoke.

Can't stop gasping in bits of Ruth's incinerate.

Long for satin ice, and pure cryogenic cold.

Not a cell left unburnt in her terminating.

My pores ashy, the nails of my fingers charcoalized.

I choke and choke in terror of catching fire, while above me, erect and undisturbed, the visored nurses stand on guard, ready to delist further.

"Ruth Perez, why did you transgress the Code?"

My mind knows only panic, an intense unknowingness, and this urgent wish to curl into sleep.

"Who performed the engram geology?"

Their eyes have been turned to glass by the power of conflagration.

My mouth, in strangled breaths, can articulate nothing but shapeless terror.

Bogdhan nods to Nikki who hooks the gun back into her belt and grasps the orange handle of the chainsaw, steps closer, hoists the machine up before my eyes and yanks on the black rubber handle that pulls out a long white cord: the whine and roar as loud as that drill operating inside my head.

Switches it off, and Bogdhan jams a knuckle under my chin: "What was your motivation in flaking off clonal croppings, and salting your brain-field with false traces?"

What explanation can I give before the racket of the chain-saw starts again, with its circling bright teeth?

Bogdhan raises a glove into the unbearable air, and silver teeth slide past my eyes.

"An experiment?" he shouts, while the other nurses watch with shielded faces.

He chops his hand down, halts the racing scream of the chain-saw, says, "In the morning we will investigate further . . ."

And I have a few seconds of hope before Bogdhan completes his sentence: ". . . by amputating a limb."

Guns and boots pivot away from me, and the nurses march out, smacking the hard floor, while the chain-saw, which shook so convulsively, rests calmly on the table.

∞

Yusef enters, the B.I.G.G. cap elevated on the pole end of a mop. He tosses the hat up in the air, catches it, then slaps the heated cap over my head, saying, "Hurry, before S.A.W. disappears you."

Remembering his moist eyes, I pull myself up, walk, totteringly, after him. Rush now from the room and its chain-saw—moving fast across the milky marble of the entrance hall until I see a tiny blue-gold hoop, scorched and solitary except that it's next to a black zero, its fixed shadow printed on the metal floor edge—and I stoop to touch the scorching metal with my combustible finger, blow through its empty space, then slip Ruth's ring around my fourth finger, and, stepping on gummy ash that leaves smudges of footprints behind, slide outside with Yusef into a cold wind and the smell of mud.

Lost now in night's imagelessness. But the beacon cores the black sky with light, and I watch elongated clouds race off into the distance, until a return to darkness.

A snuffling/growling next to my leg that is not Yusef's breathing. In terror, I must wait for the obscurity to end.

The next flash illuminates a twitching nose, floppy ears, and an open jaw. Yusef's mouth sucks and kisses in invitation to this creature which has a long tongue and hooked teeth.

The dog barks sharply into the night that too quickly has come again—senses my invisible fright. Hot slobber on my bare hand before I can snatch it away, and, almost immediately, loud crunching—recall Tom with his mouthful of ice.

The yellow beacon returns to show Yusef's black hand casually exposed, a palmful of dun pellets for the licking. The beagle wags its tail ferociously as it bites down dusty morsels of dead matter.

All of biology, tortoise, marine lizards, finches, humans, just here to ingest? I stroke the moist canine fur, and feel an unfamiliar ease while the happy beagle chews.

The sudden dark brings the loud clatter of a helicopter (that word I couldn't find sooner). Yusef jerks me forward, the dog whines, and bone-white shirts with vaporizing guns march through my brain.

And I'm grateful to the greedy night for swallowing our bodies inside its colourlessness. As the helicopter slices louder.

When the beacon pulses back on, I streak after Yusef who leaps off the sawn planks into the miasmatic earth.

I jump without thinking, and a cold, splurging overmuchness of mud squeezes up through my bare toes, covers my ankles.

Night again devours us, disappearing us into its bellied dark. Under the black scything sky I can no longer see Yusef, and must grope my way through this heavy ground by the croaking of unseen frogs, while in my brain ions repeatedly scream, "Faster!"

I squelch forward, my head a slashing, throbbing helicopter. The beacon, dangerously bright, freezes Yusef's legless body in its light.

While a tiny, blood-mad insect whirs in and out of my nose, I struggle to find footing in this cold, directionless mud that is fetid with the decay stink of skunk cabbage: my leg plunges down and is lost. Where is that serenity of an ice woman, lying on her back, dreaming of life?

Oblong outlines of holes, liquid swirls, and brown bubbles only briefly mark the bog surface I must traverse to reach Yusef who has waded too far away— his hand now raised, pushing air past his face, urging me even deeper into this yielding earth. But to shift my bloated feet, now impossible.

Yet my body, again shocked by the sharp beacon light, slurps forward, delving exhaustedly in this soft, dank place, while the beating of the machines in the sky echoes down in my chest. Squirting and sliding, I sink into puddled tracks which always vanish.

On my left leg a splotch of slime gleams, holding many tiny eggs in rounded newness—frogs yet unborn—and as my other knee goes under, I'm remembering I'm still alive. I flounder on, scared at being so disposable.

But now the helicopter sounds are fading while I plunge both my hands under the mud to wrench out a dripping brown-black leg and squelch on after Yusef—the one who helped to incise my one and only brain. He hurls his bulk forward, again and again, into muddy moreness, heaving himself towards some unseeable place beyond, while right in front of my eyes a bug with long legs strides across the smooth surface of a puddle with no effort.

Both my legs now buried, and I think of amputation. A mistake to pause, to think—as a spotted spider swims away from me with eight furry legs, I fear I will sink here, a lost nonentity.

Yusef has come part-way back, waves at me impatiently, points to something I can't discern in the darker distance beyond the beacon's reach, while a whining bug teases at my throat. Once I was untraumatized flesh with a nearly frozen brain, itchy with dreaming . . .

My mired foot flexes against a root or a dead thing, oozes on up, but soon is sunk again into one of Yusef's disappearing swirls: the grey bubbles pop and return to air-less mud. I'm breathing much too fast and moving far too slow, though my chest is jumping with wild respiration.

Under the beacon's yellow eye, my foot twists itself free from clinging earth, hovers dripping and swollen, a shapeless monstrosity. Above, a long, twisted piece of dry skin stretched out on top of the sombre, sucking mud—the sloughed-off, disregarded skin of a snake: rhomboids in three colours.

I step down, slog on, almost automatic now, my body drawn to Yusef's, like flies to the stench of dead meat in those large flowers. But one leg sinks up to my crotch, tips me sideways, and flings my arms out for something that's not just more unsupported mud.

Inside thick cold moistness my foot feels for some hidden rock, and I convulsively kick myself up, sputter desperately while my lungs clog and stretch with earth and water, until at last I get a clean bite of sky to swallow. Even here the pulsing beacon shines, lighting my webbed-in-mud hand, that looks like a fin, or a wing.

In this sick-up of mud I splash on, too tired to dread some final sinking of my unbandaged head under its muddy cap. Yusef stands monumental beneath a stringy tree, on a rocky ledge, both feet above this marshy ground.

Strangely, I don't care, and am possessed only of a lazy intensity to travel no farther. I ignore the willow leaves that rustle in my face, and merely watch his sloppy fingers strain for mine, slip off, but now they grab and tighten, elevating me to where I can stand up on two feet, like a human.

Yusef rubs circles of warmth into the near-iciness of my trembling body. Pulls me close, says, "Your cap should read B.O.G.G.," then pushes up my muddy sleeve and injects me, his hypodermic needle squirting a pale green liquid out of its numbered tube.

Was without the will to move ever again, but when Yusef begins to climb into the hilly vegetation above the swamp, I follow. Mud slops off my feet onto grasses, my heavy grey gown brushes against springy branches, and as the path starts to rise, almost vertically, our clumsy feet take short, stabbing steps, until our fatigued forms nearly down on all fours, seem to crawl beyond the beacon's light.

But above the rasp-and-whistle of my breathing, I hear the slicing of chopper blades again, and we scramble upward in the gloom. Sudden moonlight reveals a deciduous tree growing out of a log's innards.

Yusef accelerates, his boots puffing up dirt, kicking away lichen. With an adrenaline flash, I, too, lunge up the steep hillside.

At the summit I collapse on smooth stone at the very centre of some hair-line geometric markings—crying and rocking under the moon's bright yellow eye. The helicopter slashes open the sky, as the solid rock below me shudders—gives way!—and hard curved space rushes past.

∞

I curve unendingly down in wet-walled spirals. Then hard peristaltic waves clench at me. The rock dilates and I can breathe again, until the stone once more squeezes my brain, shooting out iridescent flickers. Helically winding, I now speed head-first to the earth's centre.

My fingers on the rock-smooth slipperiness of the walls are like a hurried caress, as curved space slips by. Infinitely. Pausing for a moment, but discovering no way out of falling except for intermittent rings of pressure pushing against my soft skull.

The shaft dilates, and again my expandable chest can breathe. Tantalizing fissures of light spill into the cave of my head. Speleology. But caught once more by stone shudders that come unyieldingly, in cruel waves.

Spilling and sliding again in this tunnel that winds and glistens: spelunking. Spill-uncaring. Though circumscribed by rock, and waiting for some final end. Imprisoned by slowed motion.

Stopped, clamped brainless and blacking out, with any human configuring gone. My flesh squeezed flat-and-flatter. My heart palpitating in double time. One last unbearable pressure, as I fall out into dark light.

Brained, howling, my double-damaged head takes in stony air. Under my cap (that's still on!), I feel trickling blood begin to coagulate. My eyes and electrified cortex see dim things grope towards me. In this subterranean void with only weak echoes of moonlight, they look like sawn-off limbs.

I roll my aching body over, and wish for a dreamless sleep. But black bile is in my throat, and this word, "melancholy," in my head. A loud thud beside me, and I turn to see Yusef heaped up on the limestone floor, like some giant, soft-shelled tortoise from the Galápagos. My incised, battered brain can't figure out how his body could have made the descent through that tight, unforgiving rock.

His mouth gasps, cavernously. His lungs, larynx, tongue, teeth, lips, push out a mysterious word, "pock-it," which I can't contrive into sense. Vocalizing shapeless sounds? Does "pock it" mean to make dents in something, or is the word excavated from my cache of language?

Yusef's gloved fingers tap feebly, insistently, at the fabric on his chest; his thick arm slides away to the limestone. I turn and turn the small blue-gold hoop on my finger, half-understand it's urgent for me to perform some act on his behalf. Again, his arm rises up from the rock floor, feels cross-handedly at a bulge in his shirt. I observe the gloved hand tug at a flap of cloth, go beneath it and hide, then come out holding a hard black stem, which is palpitating in his palm—

but now rolls free from his muddy fingers and flares out light.

In its clear tunnel of air, I can see matching stone forms, tapered and inanimate. None quite reaches its shining twin, though both gesture at the dankness in between, and I have a vision of myself and Ruth, my doppelgänger. We were an icicle-like pair that could never touch: one reaching down, the other growing up. Yusef, still immobilized, blows out lungbags of air.

His mauve scarf stretched, the shirt torn open, a bruise on his chest, and—where a glove finger has been ripped away, a painted nail. That vivid pink bursts in my eyes. Once more the drill rips through the curved bone of my skull, grinds in my spongy violated brain. A fury in my remembering: blood-red, string-white, wet-grey.

Yusef moans for my help; all my anger inaudible to him. In his pouched-out face, his canine teeth are bared: a laugh or a bark, beneficent or rabid? His hairy, pink-nailed finger waggles at me, but I pick up his flashlight and walk away, past a large yellow mound to a chlorophyll-green pool. There I see a pair of fascinated eyes, and, for as long as I shine the beam, my gaze gives Ruth's pear-green ones a vital warmth.

A perfect facsimile, on the surface. But not the original, just a copy, copied greenly. "Narcissism." Yusef's voice startles me—his single word that began low, then scaled up in a vibration-less dash, leaped out of my hearing in its final squeak.

Why should I care about this man's near nonexistence after he took a bite out of my head? I stare down at the face which stares unhappily out of the pool at itself. And turn the miniature blue-gold circle around my finger. On the stone lip of the pool, the light shows a small fish delicately printed, with fins like insect wings.

With the flipper bones of my hand, I lean over and touch a million-million years ago. An unliveable life. I trace the hollow for the spine, its fine fin veins, the spasms of its vague head, and feel under my finger its flutteriness, still. I recall Yusef's tap-tap-tapping on the rounded glass over flashing numbers—just before they hurt me for all my time.

Gills crushed, its fish form made invariant. A breathless image that swims eternally through rock. For how many minutes in the long fossilizing to stone did its head quiver? Its life shape immortalized by dying.

I shift Yusef's flashlight from hand to hand, turn uneasily, and walk back, listen at his closed lips. My own head not burnt to cinder air, but dizzy with loss and a chronology beyond counting. Squat to better catch his soft, irregular breath. Yusef opens his eyes, and his bare hand twitches, hesitating, unfolds to reveal a tiny package in silver foil.

Take it from him, and unwrap a yellow lozenge. My taste buds salivating at the lemon flavour. I look down on him coldly, as if his head were a site for engram geology. Watch him point desperately to his mouth, but I, like No Lips, or Bogdhan Smith, now have the power to decide what happens next—though, when his brown eyes moisten, I just drop the candy between his sucking lips, am left imagining all that sweetness he swallowed down while I lick at my sticky fingers.

Yusef's eyes are like mud on fire as he speaks, "Thanks for the medication, Ruth." A sham identity for me to live out? His voice reverberates again, "But for the trivial gain of a few fruit names, you made me act like a Nazi." That word echoes in my brain-cave, and my not knowing what it means leaves me feeling somehow subservient to this fat man lying on his back nearly lifeless.

It is as if the sounds for that word had once bounced in too quickly among my neurons, maybe when they were too busy to listen, and the meaning flashed away, and now snoozes fitful in some quiet, distant fold, but might wake up, buzzing—like that fly hitting the glass in a room where I first heard Yusef's voice coming through the wall. A *not* zee: an ending uncompleted, the last letter *not* spoken? Yusef's voice again, vibrant, telling me more things, "I guess even the first nomads bred hybrids, refashioning wild grains to feed themselves, and the first farmers tamed and fattened cattle . . . a human impulse to domesticate, to make Nature more perfectly ours, we share with the Nazis." I struggle to place his energetic twistings of words into the convolutions of my brain.

Yusef glances at his dirty, broken pink nail, and speaks with impossible gusto, "I, too, as you know, am not immune to our constant, piercing urge to *improve*, which has been our delight and doom. From tattoos to frontal lobotomies, eugenicists all: what we don't like, we cure, cut, or cull." Refashioning the world for our own use? "Not happy with the traits Mother Nature gave us, we invented pink nail polish, devised orthodenture, tit implants, nose hair scissors, steroids," and he flexes a large biceps under the flashlight I hold in my hand.

What's desirable for me? Still believes he's talking to Ruth: "Natives hinged two boards to remake the round, malleable skulls of infants into a pleasing point; the Chinese knotted feet unwalkably small; the English virtuously shifted inner organs with bone corsets. And the Nazis wearing the mask of science over hate-dreams blinded twins with searing rods, using *no* anaesthetics. But I know my speechifying bores you."

No, none of this fever of information ever seeped through the wire stuck to my nearly frozen skull. With his flashlight I nudge around the circumference of his round face, making a jerky circle of light on the limestone. "Ruth, I'm not saying I'm immune to the lures of perfection, or to the simple wish to undo unhappy reality, but to drill out a human head to mend a tiny flaw?" "Yusef, I may not look dissimilar to Ruth Perez, but I am someone else."

∞

He sits straight up, skews the brim of my cap sideways, lifts it off and delicately touches the exposed mesh. Wincing, Yusef stands, takes the flashlight from me—its glare in my face as he examines the shaved and unshaved hair on my skull. His fingers push up my sleeve, feel the raised needle marks on my arm. He pinches at my ashen, blue-gold ring, and now there's a toothy smile, and lemon on his explicating breath: "Ruth, you were just kidding me." Exterminated. And the set of my face must tell him that truth because his muddied pink nail floats up towards the stalagtitic limbs. A hot out-rush of his breath shoots down through the steel cross-wires he helped insert. He flips the cap back over the cored-out skull, and, as warm air from Yusef's body is circulating in my cold, tiny chimney, he shuffles away with the flashlight to the pool's edge where he bows his head, stares down at its mirror greenness.

He scoops up a palmful of water, pours it back, and spatters the liquid smoothness. Oblivious of me. Drops drip from the hard pinkness of his nail. I step around the heap of sulphur and watch how Yusef's cupped hand stirs the water in elliptical swirls. Why did Ruth steal a shaft of my dendrites and long axons that were meant to connect me up to this world? My million perfect neurons not joining up a fraction of a millimetre too early, or missing even the smallest linkage. Now, the firings to connect me to things across the gaps interrupted . . . Yusef rises, pats my shoulder, and enunciates very clearly: "I loved Ruth's twin sister, Lisa."

Under the flashlight the stone fish scintillates in some water splashed over the lip of the pool. What can it mean when he says he loved the sister of Ruth— who once was more than replaceable parts, and now is less? Yusef lays aside the light, and holding a curve of air below his hand, begins to talk, "Now you will have to live for three people: Lisa, Ruth, and yourself." I tremble at my new triple life, my brain sparking in chaos, remembering Ruth's airborne ash, wanting the comfort of Yusef's hand on my back. Instead, he points to the fish shape, "Base pairs in twin, spiral ladders form the genes that add up to the chromosomal lengths making up all life. Double-stranded, these chains of base pairs, which code the contours of this fish, gave shape to the proteins that bodied forth Lisa and Ruth." And where am I in this fabrication of self? Doubly-stranded?

"When stained, these banded chains that stretch and loop in our cells appear as 'colour bodies', *chromo soma*. And some years ago the Human Genome Project found out all the rungs on our chromosomal ladder, and we began building a stairway to heaven." His fingers clench and unfold, gesture at the mounded sulphur that's a lurid yellow in the cave's gloom: "That was Lisa's joke about hell-fire." I slump beside him on the pool's edge, borrow some of his heat, while he talks on to our mixed pair of greenish reflections. Yusef's voice turns hard, like ice, "Once all the ills, defects, flaws, itsy-bitsy imperfections could be tested for, then came de-selection and the cloning of the one 'Ideal' form, with the Health Code forbidding any reproductive variety. Farewell human diversity, welcome sameness. Technology let us choose the one 'perfect' fertile egg, and then let us halve this single zygote into endless identical twins—one, two, four, eight, sixteen. Hey, if chromosomes looked like coiled spaghettini, why not follow a cook book? Prepare the right ingredients *in vitro*: pick the best egg, get some superb cream sauce to go with it, and *'Bon appetite!'* Forget wild gonads when pure replication could make our dreams wake up and walk."

Yusef passes me the flashlight as his arms glide up; his muddied body rises, and now he is pirouetting, dancing. "Once Lisa took me waltzing, one-two-three-and," he sings, then leaps straight up—almost to the jagged roof—before landing, too hard, spinning imperfectly, wobbling back towards me. "Dancing revivifies the soul." Again, soaring through grey-black space— a pink nail flashing in my beam as he whirls across the limestone dangerously quick—keeping time to some unseen music, his scarf swooping off his head, like a mauve bird that flutters down to the stone. I can only watch, open-mouthed. With remarkable lightness for such a heavy man, Yusef skips over the inert cloth, swings past the sulphur pile, and clicks his boots in the dank air. Now jumps right over the green pool, lands at my feet, and takes my empty hand, and with his body hot against mine, skims away the tension from my skin, swings my flesh free, whirls away the hole in my brooding brain . . . until we stop turning. He speaks again, "Lisa fought against their Nazifying, though she, herself, was formed to be one of the 'perfect'; she saved excised traits and sneaked some 'wrong' genes back into the human pool, and was expired."

Dizzied by dancing, overloaded by these slices of information, my injured brain leaps and stumbles. "With the help of Ruth who wanted a neuron transplant to fill in a trifling gap, I was going to revive Lisa from the cell code and engram tracings." Odd rays of illumination tickle the inside of my skull, like the stray pale light that filters down to this corner of the cave. Those pink nails, her vaporizing, his flashlight, "pears," this lesion, this lesson. Yusef laughs, "The way you shift your eyes instead of your neck when you want to look at someone reminds me of Lisa and Ruth." My cheeks flush angry because his words tell me I am only a copy, and that all my thawed-out time after that long wait in the cold steel tray has been for nought, is only a dream of borrowed colours in this aching head which belongs to a self who has really lived. Yusef touches my ear gently, says, "I'm sorry; you are more than a clone." But that word, its emptying-out, makes me less, almost a blank again, though his trying to console me brings warmth to this double void of cave and skull.

But now Yusef looks away from me, beyond the green pool, past the intense yellow pile, and into the cave's blackest obscurity. He takes back the flashlight, and its beam finds a new object, a huge boulder wedged against the cave's far wall—a contrast to the vaporizing guns of the nurses that make things vanish. No slicing and rattling of a helicopter down here. His strong fingers grasp mine, and I walk with the acquisitor of my brain fruit towards the large, skull-like rock. His left leg limps slightly, dragging the mudded boot through tiny pellets of rodent scat—a welcome sign of subterranean life. "Ruth refused to help me restore Lisa to life until we fixed her verbal defect, an aphasia that seemed so trivial that B.I.G.G.'s Health Code wouldn't permit treatment. So, as you know, we grabbed your neurons, planning to replenish Ruth's brain with your names for fruits, but the damage from her skating fall must have been much worse than she thought and more traumatic than I guessed because the nurses in the Other Testing believed *she* was the clonal one— and maybe Ruth intuited some serious learning deficit, which would have resulted in the nurses carrying out a cease and desist order against her." He places both of my hands against the slick cold rock, and the flashlight falls in a clatter, leaving us in terrifying blackness.

Silent, except for our grunted breaths, we strain blindly against the boulder's curved immensity. I clutch at its wet convolutions, and feel I'm trying to move the weight of the world. Then illumination again, as Yusef snatches up the flashlight. I can see where hands press against the damp boulder, that two wrists touch as if grafted, our fingers, hairy and hairless, painted and paintless: a hermaphrodite's pair. Now his light-beam flicks away, discovering a long, rusted rod lying across a puddle. "Archimedes!" he shouts, and entrusts me with the flashlight that I grip tight while he limps off, stoops now to lift up one end of the flaking, drip-ping rod from the cave floor, then rests his heavy body on the standing metal pole, and it's disquieting (as well as pleasing) to think I may be stronger than Yusef. He brings the rod towards me, then dips its tapered end of wet orange rust under the immovable stone. All of a sudden, he's jumping up at the rod's far end, his legs flung off the ground and out of my light—high into the vague air—and the boulder ponderously begins to shift, and roll away. Yusef drops the metal rod, and there's a loud clang inside my head, and now a dense echo from its bounce. But nothing is revealed except more rock, more solidity, with the smooth cave wall sloping down to form the limestone floor.

But Yusef laughs, takes the flashlight back, tucks it into his shirt, and bends down, joining his fingers into a human step. Frozen, I stare at his linked hands, think-ing that I don't know what to think, thinking that every feeling must have a subject to feel it, and yet my know-ing my knowing to be only an echo of Ruth's brain puts me on the outside from what's inside my "own" head, and I am a stranger to myself, since the "I" which I pronounce can't be *my* self, even as "I" must decide what to do. Yusef still waits, bent over, his hands with interlacing fingers down there, and my dirty foot here. My muddy brain belongs to an inner Ruth, though ultimately I differ from her because I resent being only her shadow. . . His hand touching my shoulder, Yusef swirls the flashlight to reveal two metres up, a penetrable wound. By placing the whole weight of my bones and flesh in Yusef's hands, it's conceivable I could spring up that high and hurl my head into the stone gap, but is it an entrance or an exit? He again gives me the flashlight to hold, and I place my cold foot in his cupped hands—but with Yusef down below, would I be stranded and solitary, in an unknown passage to nowhere, at a dead end? He nudges my foot and I leap, thrusting my wired head into darkness, and with an agonized hand grab at the slipping insides of the small tunnel while my legs dangle.

Yusef shoves my foot, catapulting me up to where I can drag my knees safely inside. Scooting in deeper, I'm a fearful caver, a scared spelunker who can't see her own hand, until I click the flashlight on. Yusef yells, and I look back to the tunnel's mouth, and shine the light down to illuminate Yusef as he runs in a frenzy with the long, rusted rod slung out from his waist, pointing up at me, before it dips out of view, and I hear a scraping, grinding noise, and see his body coming at me, feet-first. I scrabble into the unknown blackness while just behind me there's a heavy thud, the scuff of sliding boots, a loud, dull clang, and now out-of-control laughter. The deep delight bouncing out of his reverberant chest feels as good as his hands rubbing warmth into my body. Yusef hugs me, takes the light, squeezes past, and is bounding ahead into the next black curve. His probing flashlight flares against the damp tunnel stone, brightly apportioning our future.

But then his broad back interposes, gets between my eyes and the shining as we descend into moist, prehistoric staleness. I hear dripping, and image the non-fish shape of my body fossilizing under the weight of earth above me. A scared vision of my ribs pressed flat, their curving branches that felt the flutter of wind in lungs buried eternally in layers of sunless rock: an imprint of an imprint. A trickle from the stone roof splashes on Yusef's exposed neck, and my foot skids on slipperiness. Lurching, I clutch at a milky leg-like stone before I straighten up—find we're in a surprisingly broad chamber. Yusef reaches down, picks up a small triangular stone that glows darkly under his light. "Obsidian," he says, hiding the flaked arrow head in the pouch with a button on his shirt: ("pocket.")

On the stone wall in front of us is a wounded beast, its back curved taut, and the head with its open eye curled tight against its hoofs. "Part of the magic of staying alive was drawing a picture of a bison to kill, and then hurling actual spears at the pigments. With the technology of guns and bombs, the magic of killing became too easy: now you see it, now you don't. And if Mother Nature had now become mortal, why not plastic limbs, baboon and metal hearts, or fetal seed cells for dried-out brains thirsting for dopamine? Why not go for eternity through reincarnation: cloning?" Because then I am only here for someone else's use, a spare body of colour: a chromosomal slave. I ask, "What about the hooked arm with pink nails?" His voice swallows itself, and Yusef speaks unevenly, "I worked at the hospital where the Board in Genome Governancing admitted Lisa for extinction, and I managed to smuggle her sawn-off arm out of the ward, so that we. . . . Listen, the nurses could arrive down here any second, so I can't tell you the whole story right now."

Yusef averts his face, and we swerve out of the wide chamber, back into the tunnel that contracts as we climb—forcing us to crouch forward (claustrophobic), the skin of my arm against damp rock. An overhanging stone brushes my cap, so I hunch down even more. Yusef, stuck momentarily in a narrow turning, breaks free with a bellow, and I begin to listen for the echoes of the nurses' boots. Silent, crouching, I follow Yusef once again, mimic the shapings and manoeuvrings of a body unlike mine. And always, my dendrites, cortex, synapses, ions, the cerebellum that reports and instructs my body on how to move in this cramped space, all of me, responds to the probing yellow eye of his flashlight. Remembering those images of watery eyes in sockets of dim-white . . . black lips. Why not just lie down here and rest, a satiated length of life on cold grey stone, instead of moving on with my form bent like a question mark, or an upside-down hook? I desire no more of this perpetual pursuit of the next dark zone beyond *this* curve and hollow.

But Yusef is gradually growing taller, and air blows fresh against my face. Almost at full height now, Yusef stops, and I wait, behind him, eager and bored and anxious, gazing at all this rock that contains us, and I wonder if it is the mutilation of my brain that makes my mind always look for words to describe myself to myself. His head sideways to the stone, he listens at a slit of light, turns and gives me the flashlight with its compact weight, saying, "I could alphabetize a universe of things that you need to know, but we don't have time." Is he abandoning me? His hand reaches for my face, wavers in front of my eyes, squeezes my shoulder; as I turn, his fingers gently trace out the length of my spine, feeling all the double bumps from brainstem to tailbone before his deep voice flows out: "Amino acids, animals, alleles, Adolph Hitler, Achilles, abortion, Amerika, amniocentesis, AIDS, anticodons, Africa, antisense strands, aesthetics, Adam and Eve, auto-representation, Alzheimer's, anabolic steroids, and alkaptonuria where pee turns black in the air." I'm baffled by the velocity of his words which blur all meanings, but I like his hand rubbing warmth into my body. Yusef's voice tumbles on: "Base pairs, botany, the Bach family, bigotry, a boy in a plastic bubble, beautification, bacteriophage, the Beagle, Bikini Atoll." I click off the light by mistake, but he barely pauses for a new breath: "Cancer, chimeras, cryogenics and clones." A flash of futile rage and I shine the beam at Yusef's brown eyes, but his ragged voice goes on through its odd, crowded list to some unknown end: "DNA and Down's syndrome, and Darwin and daguerreotypes, and Dolly, and, of course, the big 'D', Death, eugenics, fruit-flies and favourable traits, grafting, hemophilia, horse races, and homophobia, the insurance industry or icon or IQ, jumping along a chromosome, Kafka, Luria, Mendel, mutations and monozygotic twins, Narcissus or Nagasaki, orangutans, Plato, purines, and *pears*, quasicrystals of 500 bases for DNA sequencing, royalty, riflips, and racism, Southern blots and sexism, Tay-Sachs disease and transgenic mice, Utopia, vaccines, Watson, James D.'s double helix or even Watson, friend of the famous sleuth, X-ray crystallography, youthfulness, and zygotes, all end where you began."

Yusef's breath hot and sweet on my face. But too many names and things flicked at my inadequate brain. His half-turned chest swells and falls under my beam, and the dark brown epidermis glows through a rip in his shirt like a patch of moonlit earth. "As the illegally fertilized egg of a nurse and a cook, I must resume my janitorial mode." He closes his two index fingers against the corresponding thumbs, and then joins these two shapes to form a squished, sideways number eight, or a pair of blank eyes. "Wait here until you see this signal, then cross the field after me. If I don't signal, *run* back through the tunnel, squeeze yourself up that damned sausage-grinder of a rock chimney, and, if the nurses aren't guarding the exit, hustle back down the hill to the bog. When you face the S.A.W. building, bear left . . . and create a new path."

Yusef, lightly (intimately?) covers the back of my hand with a gloveless hand, presses down, shuts off the flashlight, and slides his body out into the grey-pink air. At the cave's half-mouth, I watch the fog of his breath blowing back at me, in cool, crepuscular gusts that promise neither sun nor night: I can't tell what will be next. Head hunched, body held low, Yusef is now in a field of flinging stalks and furled, bent leaves, while wind whistles feverishly at my face here in the tunnel's gap. My thumb twitches on the flashlight, wanting to throw light out to catch the black bobbing head disappearing among the high plants. Each step takes Yusef further into the shelter of growing things, farther from this dark flashlight and my muddied self, left solitary except for the endless natter and constant doubling into words inside my hurting head. Impossible now to see him at all, let alone his signal. The wind in its piercing like hypodermic needles. I tell my fingers which grip the flashlight unfeelingly not to squeeze out light, and Yusef's head emerges at the far end of the field, and his hands rising in the pink-grey light with the sign for infinity.

Scraping against mildewed rock, I swing myself outside in a half-arc, halt, and try to hug my undecided body warm. My brain has again copied itself into language, and as I wait I'm trying to guess at consequences, deciding how to decide, trying to find words that aren't too short or too long, some language that would fit my life. Yusef, impatiently, lets go of his linked, flattened eights, and his arms fall out of sight. To cross into this blowing green field that becomes clearer in what must be sunrise will only carry me to some further place from which I will again have to decide to move on, going always beyond a place of knowledge into a site of my imagining. Maybe if I had a name, I could sense a heading, be oriented, or at least feel some hint of heat in my toes. Indecisive. But remembering the clinging cold earth of the swamp, how can I not risk new fatigue and unknown fears? A piece of grit is irritating my eye; Yusef's bare hand beckons for the last time.

My feet step towards him, even before the remains of my brain have figured out there's no alternative. And now I'm hidden and lost among tall plants whose heavy, green-sheathed cylinders have silky tassels. By my toes, a discard with tiny empty sacs in endless rows and, near one end, small yellow teeth: a fruit or a vegetable for which I have no word. To make nil, to annihilate, as with Ruth, implies a more than nothing to start with, not just a thawed copy. But how can I cross over to newness by replicating Yusef's footfalls? Though now he is riding something, folded over a speeding black object that reverberates inside my head, its two wheels spinning so fast they appear still. Don't want him to leave me alone, at least until I have enough words to make a pattern for myself that's as clear and strong as the painted bison, and I start running along the narrow lanes of hard-packed soil, my clenched hands punching at the wind, my legs pounding—lift-bend-stretch-land. Needing more word pigments to visualize a future with, I streak past the blowing green stalks.

Breathless, I come out of the field just as Yusef corners his low-slung machine, throwing off gravel, and races right at me. My body leaps back among the yellow-teethed plants. In a skid of small stones, Yusef stops, takes the flashlight I still carry, and pulls me up after him onto the . . . onto (word delay) . . . onto the motorcycle. We thrust forward, vaporizing the world! I'm grabbing at his flesh and ribs—and at my cap—as Yusef grins gapped-toothed, shouts, "We can outrun helicopters!" His arms shake at both ends of the wide metal handle, and he yells out a long word which eludes me in the wind, the crunch of gravel, and the automatic sounds—and we go airborne, bounce, slew sideways, and ride on. "It's a banned substance that makes humans crash and fly!" I snuggle and shelter behind his body, scared by how much I love this engine throbbing under us, and Yusef shouts again, "Testosterone!" as we blast over a hill.

When the road curves, we lean towards the dawn, straighten up, and careen towards a sky whose pink skin is being scraped off. I look past Yusef's shoulder into a wind that jabs at my eyes, makes them horizonless; I shut them, and smell diesel and fruit. My B.I.G.G. cap blows off, tumbles back there with the fumes, and

I think (with guilt) of my double, Ruth, who has liberated me by her going, who has left me free to travel on this open road between soft, growing fields as one who is more than a cloned nothing. Yusef brakes, skids, now doubles back, riding towards the cap, snatches it from the road's ditched edge, and shoves the peaked cloth inside his shirt, but no way for him to recover the one he "loved," to retrieve the frozen cells of Lisa's arm (which must be exactly the same as mine). We can wheel about on the gravel, but there's no road back in time, no re-membering of Lisa's dangling limb after Chen's lab was blown up. My identity must be that of a twin—or triple—absence. The mechanical whine becomes lower as we twist and climb past scattered pines, and the front wheel shudders against a rock, bounces off, and we're on a new line of descent, zooming down a bend, making the landscape liquid, while geography flows past us—pours like water or blood through my hands. Both twin sisters, with their billions of scorched and crushed cells, live on in my body.

But this morning I have travelled one full night beyond Ruth's nonexistence. As the tires thrum, revolve on even, tarry pavement, and we move beside the shelter of a grassy hill, I am now an ex-clone, aware that the bits of events in my life have taken me somewhere beyond nothing, and that I should be happy and careless of our destination in the new day's warmth, but I poke my finger into Yusef's soft back, ask, "Where?" His head shakes, signifying deafness. I scream over the motorcycle's noise into the dark shining seashell of his ear: "Where?" Yusef's head again spasms into silence, my wish to know thwarted. Must any understanding of where I'm headed come only *after we have arrived*, when it's too late? At the end of the journey, what use is the mind's retroactive freezing of lived moments into something that can be made to look like a design? Down below, the road seems to fall off, and double arcs shimmer silver and span a blue-grey river.

The pavement leads us out onto the bridge, and the motorcycle bumps over wooden planks which show strips of river below. Yusef steers us back onto smoothness, then twists the motorcycle off the road, stopping our forward motion on a patch of dirt, digging his right foot down for balance. He shuts off the engine, and, when he turns, all the muscles of his face have gone cryogenic. At last his lips open, "I can't hide you from the nurses," and I look at the river, search for motion there, find along the edge, away from its smooth centre, a few unimportant movements, some quiet swirls, darting insects, bubbles, and a broken stick that catches on some reeds before it drifts downstream. But I can't see any unfossilized fish swimming. Yusef's chin tightens up as he scans the morning sky—looking for helicopters? Warm air rustles-rustles through a nearby field of green plants with those hidden yellow teeth, and stirs the river's surface. He tells me, "You will have to hope the winds of chance blow your way."

My brain sees gills flapping in air, petrifying, and Ruth's face molten, her body turning to soot. A pair of teal-necked ducks splash in the river while I wait, my bum itchy on the hot black seat of the motorcycle, and I twist the band around my finger. Half-consciously, I pull the ring off, rub at the ash, spit on the metal, wipe and polish with the sleeve of my gown, then hold its brightness up—look inside where four inscribed letters flash in the sun: "AtGo." I ask him, "What's the significance?" Yusef chuckles, "It was another one of Lisa's jokes, a tiny variation on the four bases which form the pairs that sequence and build the chains of proteins we're made from: adenine, thymine, guanine, and cytosine, A, T, G, C, with that last letter that she closed into a circle, 'O' to hold everything, or to signify nothing. For Lisa and I, it was a way to remember, a way to forget the one fixed genotype imposed as the Ideal, so those initials became our love letters, and also later, the name for our secret 'band' which was going to return humans to gene freedom, to that happy and unhappy chaos there at the beginning, when our species was 'at go.'" I slip the ring back on, wonder about human shapes, sizes, and colours, ask Yusef: "Why do the nurses with their visors up have so many different appearances?" "Before the Code prescribed one single Form, we evolved with different traits because Nature likes variety, and change. That's probably why we're still suckers for fashion, but on the road to this Utopia it was pretty much decided we should only worship one zygote: yours."

"Do you mean most people are like me?" He again looks into the glare of sky, "No, there are big limits to this gene egalitarianism, since those of us who mop the floors, take out the garbage, obey orders like the custodial staff of nurses, have random genes, and are needed for a lot of reasons, one being to remind the identical Equals of what it is to be imperfect. Out of despair with history, sameness had been agreed upon as a drastic cure for xenophobia. A few survivors of the brief war of nuclear ethnic cleansing argued for xenophilia, but the more pragmatic voices won out, stressing that love for others happened *rarely*, while most humans didn't hate themselves enough to commit suicide." Once I wanted to kill Ruth Perez, my dopplegänger. "Some wanted to de-genderize the world, eliminate all males, who seemed programmed for war, but the compromise worked out was to keep some men around and make the one 'perfect' form of the Equal *female*, with back-up copies like you in the clonal warehouse, whose emblem became an absence, a missing belly button." I slide forward into the driver's seat, and squeeze the ends of the metal bar. "Heterosex, of course, became a crime, but, naturally, some babies, like myself, were born with scattered genes out of the helter-skelter of desire. The Equals get to determine what is safety and wellness, but they can't always control their own sex lives, let alone ours."

"Yusef, if you are not a Nazi, why did you take part in my mutilating?" His face swirls and bubbles, his mouth a caught stick twisting free slowly: "Out of love. Of course I could have restored Lisa's body from a single cell in her arm. Or from yours. But because B.I.G.G. had hours of her interrogation in electronic files, which Ruth had access to, I planned to re-transcribe those linguistic taces into her brain. Hoping to recreate at least a half-life for my Lisa. Maybe with coaxing and coaching. I wanted badly to bring her back from the dead.

"Like Orpheus. But if my song had managed to charm Death, it would have been made up of my beloved's own words." I'm her sister, too, the one he loved, the Lisa who danced, the one whose pink nails were my horror and solace—my bit of a friend crushed by the plexi-faced nurses. I swing my body off, burning my thigh on the hot metal of his motorcycle. If my identical twins are Lisa and Ruth, or Ruth and Lisa, then what about Reisa as a name? I walk on the round stones by the river's edge, wade into the cold, clear water until the downstream flow tugs at me, bloating out my grey gown, making me hemispheric. Yusef splashes in beside me, and the two of us billow out like sails, and I see the mud and cave dust wash off the grey fabric and feel I could float away with my new name. He dips and rinses my cap in the river, says, "I just had a novel idea."

A minnow bumps its nose against my ankle, and my shadow on the water's surface is that of a very fat person bursting with laughter. His gentle hand washes stiff mud off my clothes, and from my face (tender?), then he pauses, while the back of his hand shades the sun: "Do you hear anything?" No, but Yusef is churning towards land, his pants now dripping on the shore stones, as he splooshes over to his motorcycle, squelches down on it, and starts it running with a loud pop. He's flawed, and I'm nameless, and meant to be nothing but accessible parts. Should I just paddle out to the river's deepest part, and dive my body into its darkest wetness and let the downstream tug take me away? Yusef shouts, "You'd better shake a leg." I kick my leg out through the dense water and vibrate my foot in the hot air. Broken-breathed sobs come from his mouth, and I realize he's laughing at me.

Irritated, I hide my head in the cool water: my open eyes see the dark silver blur of a small fish. When I lift my face out to breathe, I hear Yusef, shout, "No, no, it's just a saying," his palms opened out to me. I nod, begin moving the heavy water aside with my legs until I can walk effortlessly through air, and stride in my gown that's dark with water over to the hot gas tank with its painted flames of yellow, orange, and burning red. With Ruth's clean ring on my washed hand, and the one-two-three-and of Lisa's waltzing in my head, I am *at go*. Yusef touches my elbow as I swing myself on back of the motorcycle that sputters under me, and I tell him: "My name is Reisa." Yusef revs the engine loudly, says, "I'm pleased to meet you, Reisa, and your destination is the Igloo." I *won't* go back to that place of frozen replication when I could be Reisa, riding off into sunlight, as soon as his hand rotates the throttle and vaults us forward, vaporizing time. And we do accelerate into a swerving ride, my fragrant flesh fully at one with itself, and with my twin sisters it copies.

No helicopters from the Ruth-less world of S.A.W. follow us. My torso softens, grows languid in the jouncing heat as Yusef takes us through the curves, but the two small mirrors in front on the steering bar show where we have been an instant before, and he hurries me back to my pre-existence, a frigid cave of shadow selves. Now he guides the motorcycle onto the long straight road with its double row of tall trees. Again, my eyes strain to make the two lines join at some far point near infinity. Ruth once wheeled me down here beneath wet clouds to the dark shed, my skin thawing. I wonder if for the Equals, too, meaning has to be a looking back that's not distinct from regret. The motorcycle speeds the individual trees into blurry lines, which begin to feel like walls. My stomach tightens as we rush down this stone path to a dome with reflecting silver windows.

I *refuse* to return to the Igloo. Leaning far forward, I yank at one of the rubber handle ends, and before

Yusef can jerk it back, we've careened off the roadway, lurched over tree roots, the engine stalling in a field with green sprouts. "You're as willful as your sisters!" "I won't be a frozen clone again." "If not, you'll be flamed and disappeared." No worse than ice in a steel tray. "Reisa, listen to me, and put this B.I.G.G. cap back on so you'll be able to walk past the nurses who guard the Igloo, and. . . ." "No," I shout, hopping off his motorcycle.

Yusef gets off too, starts digging in the ground, tugs at some green sprouts. "Reisa, let me tell you about this guy who spent his time thinking about how laughter demolished fear by bringing the world so close you could upend it, turn it inside out, break its shell open, and look into its very centre." Yusef jabs his pink nails into the earth. "This guy, whose leg was cut off, lived in exile in a vast frozen place under an ogre who constantly threatened to kill him." Not sentient ice. "This guy knew laughter kept ideas from being frozen into unreal things." Yusef heaves out a long, tapering orange thing before my amazed eyes. "He wanted each person to dig out her own sense from the old ground of language planted by strangers, and make words utterly new."

He dangles this strange, earth-flecked object with translucent strings in a hypnotizing swing. "Every word spoken, Reisa, should be a starting again, an answer, or a question, a re-stating, an ironic echo, a dialogue with all the people who have spoken that word before, so nothing can ever be frozen as *final*, and so others in the history of the future will, in turn, speak our dead words from their own places with fresh tones, in dialogue with us, utter newly." Yusef astonishes me by shoving the pointed orange thing into his mouth and biting down so hard he severs it in two. He rolls the amputated bit on his tongue, and swallows. "Reisa, at any moment a word can change its meaning in dialogue, so any self-definition has a 'loophole', and even Equals can become ambiguous and elusive to themselves." How, then, can a non-clone be categorized? "This guy, Mikhail Bakhtin, his leg amputated, at a time of famine, slaughter, conformity, and silence, needing his wife to make rag animals to buy food with, writes about laughter, then rolls his paper words up into cigarettes and smokes all his brilliant thoughts to ashes, drinks tea and waits, perhaps dreaming up our future voices that would continue his dialogue and know of an openendedness that puffs away despair. When alone, with no one to talk to, we keep turning words over in our heads, imagine conversations in our brains as a kind of rehearsal for what might come, and in this mute exchange of words and made-up voices we stay human, and alive."

Yusef's fist shoves the thing's hurt end—a pure and undirtied orange—at my lips, and when I lurch away, he laughs, not understanding my horror. "It's just a carrot," he says, a word and concept uninserted in my brain, or scooped out. Now he realizes, "I'm sorry, but it's easy to forgot you're . . ." "My name is Reisa Bakhtin." "O.K., Reisa Bakhtin, my name is Yusef Tremblay, and you probably have a verbal deficit for vegetables because the quarrying was done nearby for the fruit words lacking in Ruth's brain." My mind knows of the grouping, "vegetable," but it is a null set, with no members. "If you go back to the Igloo, you might survive, continue *becoming* through words and

211

laughter, which doesn't mean some stupid linear dream of progress or just talking in circles, but speaking like a human in a long, long dialogue, though Reisa, right now, we had better shake a leg." Spontaneous shakings in my chest, noisy air pushing up and wheezing out through my slack-jawed mouth, I find I am laughing.

"Carnivalesque," he says, chomping down on the carrot, and tosses away the green hairs. "The carrot for going back to cryogenic form is the chance for an unfrozen future." Happy to be here, sharing a joke with Yusef, and covering up the hole in my head with this cross-hatch of language. "The stick, the nurse's decomposing guns." Carrots scare me, but Ruth's burning . . . "Stay in the Igloo for awhile, and our AtGo gang will figure out how to rescue you more permanently." I nod my assent, and he pulls the B.I.G.G. cap down tight over this head of mine. "O.K., Reisa, first, you need to take off Ruth's ring because it identifies you as an outlaw." Don't want to, and I turn it around and around on my finger, then I slide it off and give it to him quick, and he just drops it into the hole in the sprouting field where the carrot grew, and tosses two handfuls of earth over the tiny, blue-gold circle.

"Reisa, at the entrance to the Igloo, walk past the nurses without pausing or looking back." Or looking at the vaporizing weapons that can make me less than ice. "Go directly to the room of replicated forms, to the very end of the line of trays, grab one of the clones, and lug it back to the empty tray you used to lie on." How can he talk so unfeelingly of my former self, of an "it"? "Switch gowns with it, and put the B.I.G.G. cap on its head, then run back down the line of clones to the newly vacant tray, stretch out there, attach the wire

to your brain, and pull the metal hood over your head."
So instead of me, *it* will be annihilated. "No, Yusef, it
would feel like prearranging my own murder." "There's
no other way of staying alive, of making up a future,
and for that one clone gone, Reisa, you might give birth
to many new lives."

∞

My nipples tender with sudden desire for an infant's
mouth, for a self that's more than a blank echo, for a
womb teeming with eggs, and I'm abundantly fertile
with hope because a child from the unselected genes
of wild sex fluids might wake into being truly alive—
and do I sense a blood itch for Yusef inside my Lisa-
like self?—and I want to start what has no end, so I
nod, but am still unhappy to switch a body just like
mine, and he says, "You must walk to the Igloo as if
you had never been fabricated and stored there," and
I'm collapsing on him, the full weight of my flesh in
his arms before he swings me back onto the hot motorcycle seat, and his hand dabs at some dirt on my
cheek, saying, "Remember Bakhtin's last word,
'unfinalizability,'" and he now half-lifts me off the machine in a hug that squeezes my breath away, then
waves me off as I stare down at where the ring is buried before I duck under some branches and step back
onto the road and begin walking towards the giant
dome where the double lines of trees nearly converge,
and notice that my gown has become a lighter colour
again under the drying sun and looks almost like it did
originally, and pull down the peak of my cap, trying to
walk stiffly upright so I look taller and change my foot-

213

fall on the hard surface from a scuff and a shuffle to a quick slap, but at the thought that I must kill a mirror likeness of myself, I slow, stop, glance over my shoulder at the blank stretch of pavement behind me, with the doubling of trees that extends almost endlessly in that other direction too, and I imagine all my twin sisters who are frozen and doubled and redoubled into hundreds or maybe thousands, and I look for Yusef and his motorcycle, but he is nowhere, and I could stop and cry, but instead feel I'd better shake a leg before the nurses saw it off.

My head turns towards the Igloo with the large silver windows that block back the morning light, and I'm walking into my frozen past while I'm talking to myself about making up a future as I go along, trying to conceive what it would be like to conceive with Yusef's fleshed bone inside my moistness—his laughter waltzing this body away which used to be just a block of ice belonging to the Board in Genome Governancing—dreaming of an act inconceivable with one of those visored nurses who stand there in bone-white shirts, sharp zig-zag teeth blood-red on their chests, and weapons held in spotless gloves, and I'm talking to myself (in silence) since I am Reisa Bakhtin and no longer impersonating Ruth Perez, I don't think, though I'm pretending to the status of an Equal, when I hear the growl of a motorcycle behind me, but I don't pause because there's slippery funk in my armpits as I approach the double oval doors, and the flared steel held by the nurses swings towards me as they train on the throaty sounds coming from the motorcycle behind my back, and under this sun that's nearly right over my head their two pale blue helmets gleam with indifference, as the building looms immense, and the engine now, a racketing pulse, and I'm still strides away from the double doors of the warehouse wall when Yusef and his wheeling machine explode into airborne black bits in a phosphorescent sky that darkly rains down in my hot imagination only, but I can't look back, and march on, sweating, trying to ignore the flared ends of weapons, one of which, rider-high, points for a long second at my heart, before my genetic matter moves on, between the two guard nurses, and now beyond their white boots, and I can at last turn my face to see Yusef slowing up, cornering, looping back, and riding casually free, while I, Reisa Bakhtin, slip into the Igloo as into a loophole, step back into this cold, scent-less air, and walk across the hall to where I can push at a shut door which swings sharp light in, and I'm the one now, though not a nurse, standing on this bright wedge of floor in front of a large cell of dim forms, my shadow at my feet, and I am frozen here by the insubstantiality of all these ones like me who are waiting, outside of time.

∞

Running now past metal frames in dark greyness to the room's end wall where I lift a chrome bowl off a cold skull and pop the wire from the scalp and lug a like-bodied self towards the open door and the blue light switch and just hurry up but her feet drag and faster and dopple-dopple-doppelgänger and flop it up onto the waiting tray and it's me was me is was is me and talking to myself when I need to shut the open door and close out the light and changing and tangling gowns and tearing and I can't annihilate something that's nothing so I run and bump and grope my way back to the newly empty bed and try to become just a clone again because I will be nothing and nothing if S.A.W. finds out and I Reisa Bakhtin forgot to attach its wire and must once more race through charcoal air towards the door where my hands feel at a cold head like mine and I pop the wire onto its brain and shove the B.I.G.G. cap down to its ears and return past rows of white teeth to stick the wire back into my own brain and pull on the chrome hood to hide the shaven circle on my icing head and am waiting and why did Ruth feed me soup and it's not alive and just a nought and what did Yusef mean when he said he loved Lisa and I'm here and alive but I want to save my shadow self so I unstick myself again and get off the freezing tray and rush to the doorway where I flick on the big blue switch and she has a face that is mine with ice crystals on her brows and staring pear-green eyes that make me look away from its gaze towards a narrow inner door that opens to show a mop and a bucket and a folded blanket on a wide shelf and maybe the nurses won't look in there so I twist and lift and slide and heave the chilled body up there and wrap it in the heavy red squares of wool with the braided fringe tickling my lips before I slam the cupboard door and flick off the light and hurry back into my prone position and wait and wait for the AtGo rebels to rescue me having tried to save it when a knock bruises my ears which I cover trying to warm my cold lobes but dreading the searing whoosh of vaporizing bone that left Ruth's blue-gold ring to enclose nothing but transparency or earth so I feign sleep but there is again knocking from the closet by someone like me who is my base pair and only a shadow's shadow who should just go back to the hard inconsequentiality of ice so I won't burn with perplexity about what she wants besides out and I wait hoping the room's silence will lengthen and I can forget any dialogue because it and I will be nothing and nothing if S.A.W. finds out and I thought they'd have burst in by now as I wait for more knocking from the one I unplugged and replugged to the wire feed and hid and now I partly long for her signals or words in this Igloo murk but also calculate that by this time my companion must have lapsed back into its cryogenic state in which case it wouldn't cry or even mind if I took her red plaid blanket for my shivering body but if I opened the closet door to find it awake and wrapped in wool waiting to get out then I would have to push her back in and wait it out in this silent cold where I risk talking to myself forever among hundreds of grey congealed bodies that haven't even had a half-life in their one Equal form that is co-identical with mine in this dizzying echo of inert matter in the parallel trays except that the brains of these clones have not been quarried and they wait in an ignorance that is complete and perfect except for their wishes which I know of well and some other things too though I know I couldn't find that word for the carrot that Yusef twisted out of the ground and amputated with his teeth or for those sheathed cylinders of yellow teeth even yet but I wonder how or if an unalive clone could *mind* if I used a few of its unused neurons to make myself whole again and I might persuade Yusef to insert them into my numbing skull by telling him it would compensate for his drilling out my brain and "harm" to a nonexistent

217

thing maybe doesn't *matter* in the scheme of worldly
things or else we might create newly in the shape of a
baby if he inserted himself there in my tender lower
gap to join us as one creature whose two tense curves
would moan in the thick stink dust of pollen with a
wet heat where my legs meet and so my eyes pulse and
dot in orange-reds and blacks like the shiny rounded
carapace of a ladybug winging open but I fear what
might flower ("yes") in my womb after the violent
breaths and that such a human life might differ from
my perfect dreaming of it through words in my brain
and could wake with a monstrous head stitched green
like a brute human but I guess I am a clone again and
I'm beginning to doubt I've ever left this cold room
which holds too much nought and I'm starting to believe there is just ice with none of its clone word "jus-
tice" which is made up from two parts but is not like a
frozen zygote in endless mirrors and I lie here and listen for a voice from the cupboard and long for it to
knock against my consciousness once more but in this
ice silence I can only dream again of exit or better yet
imagine many exits with myself leading a revolt of all
these cold selfs into the warm outside air at last but I
fear the nurses swinging their immaculate weapons
inside with the sharp light of the door and in this cold
cell where all laughless time freezes into dread I mutely
wait fearing this is a dream within a dream though I
seem really to be turning back into ice as my eyes seem
to watch a moving circle woven of stems each with
twin pears that have a large bite out of every one and
it's been a long time since I've heard anything from
the one in the cupboard with the blanket made of the
same material as Yusef's mauve scarf that he must have

forgotten back on the cave floor beside the pool with the still body of a fish printed in stone and I am starting to ache again with too much nought in this airless air and I might get up again and peek in at the one in the cupboard or hug her tight or maybe we could just warm each other with words when all at once light that is not day swings in and this is not I don't think don't think now a dream coming true though it might be Yusef and the AtGo gang dancing in and and

About the Author

Keith Harrison studied at U.B.C. (Honours English), California (Berkeley), and McGill (Ph.D., Dean's Honours List). His dissertation was "Malcolm Lowry: "This Weight of the Past." In addition to half a dozen essays on Lowry, he has written several critical articles on such writers as Bakhtin, Barthes, Byron, Samuel Hearne, Patrick Lane, Pat Lowther, Marquez, Ian McEwan, Ondaatje, and Shakespeare. Also, he has composed more than a dozen ciné-fiches for the National Film Board of Canada, primarily on Canadian writers, and has published articles on film. Harrison has published three novels, *Dead Ends* (Quadrant Editions, 1981), *After Six Days* (Goose Lane Editions, 1985), and *Eyemouth* (Goose Lane Editions, 1990). *Dead Ends* was a finalist in the Books in Canada First Novel Award. *Eyemouth* was a finalist for QSPELL's Hugh MacLennan Fiction Prize. He teaches English and Creative Writing at Malaspina University-College, and lives on Hornby Island.